THE DIVINE COMEDY

A COLLECTION OF SHORT STORIES AND MICROFICTIONS

SHUBORNO CHAKROBORTY

Made with ♥ on the Notion Press Platform
www.notionpress.com

To my Loving Family, Through the highs and lows, you have remained by my side, offering solace during moments of doubt and celebrating every milestone with unbridled joy. Your unwavering faith in my abilities has fueled my determination to pursue my dreams and push the boundaries of my creativity.

To my Experiences, you have been the reason behind both the highs and lows in my life. Your majestic way of testing me by pushing me through the fire of emotional turmoil and seemingly hopeless situations has helped me make a comeback each time with greater wisdom and learning than before. I eagerly await more such trials.

Contents

Contents

Contents

Acknowledgements

I would like to express my deepest gratitude to my beloved brother, Shubham Chakraborty. Your consistent support and constant motivation have been instrumental in bringing this book to fruition.

I would like to acknowledge the painstaking effort and dedication of those who have supported me in refining this collection. To the individuals who took the time to go through every story, offering valuable feedback and insights, your guidance has been invaluable.

To my family and friends who have believed in me and cheered me on throughout this process. Your presence in my life has been a constant source of strength and encouragement. Without the collective efforts and support of all these incredible individuals, this book would not have been possible.

To my readers, this book is a culmination of the experiences I have lived and the lessons I have learned along the way. Each story is a reflection of the myriad emotions and experiences that have fuelled my creativity. It is an expression of the triumphs, challenges, joys, and sorrows that have shaped my journey.

Thank you,
Shuborno Chakroborty

Short Stories

In this compelling section, the stories traverse diverse realms, embracing absurdity, magical realism, dreams, family dynamics, politics, and spirituality. They peel back the layers of human relationships, offering profound insights into the complexities of family dynamics, mental health, political landscapes, and societal intricacies. Prepare to embark on a multifaceted journey where imagination knows no bounds, where each narrative intricately weaves the fabric of the human experience. As you turn the pages, you'll find yourself immersed in worlds both familiar and fantastical, where the boundaries of reality blur, and the essence of the human experience takes center stage.

CHAPTER ONE

THE DIVINE COMEDY

Gods were both terrified and flabbergasted to witness their chief enchanted by a new invention created by the lowly humans. The sole topic of discussion among the divine beings residing in the city of gods revolved around this astonishing development. No one could fathom why the all-powerful being, who possessed the ability to create a multitude of universes, would become so engrossed in a basic invention crafted by the humans inhabiting a small blue planet traversing one of these universes within the multiverse created by the chief himself. The chief guarded access to this invention exclusively, denying anyone in the kingdom the privilege of using "The Generative AI."

The chief remained secluded in his room throughout the day, causing great concern among his attendants. The opulent halls buzzed with criticism from the staff members. The creative team felt the chief's absence for weeks, contemplating engaging in political maneuvers without first understanding the cause. Meanwhile, the maintenance team sat idle, and the implementation team, typically the busiest, struggled to implement the final output from the creative team. Gravitation, their brainchild, had led them to adopt a net-like space-time model, making them masters of macro-level implementation. The creative team, too, had an impressive body of work. However, a dispute erupted within the team while finalizing the human brain. One member advocated for simple intelligence, basic survival fitness, and awareness akin to other animals, while another argued for enhanced human intelligence, a moderate level of awareness with an option for upgrades, and a high survival ability. This disagreement led to a feud, with the majority of the team voting for improved abilities. This irked the dissenting member, who, before departing, introduced a self-destruct code by inducing various emotions in humans, along with the mind-brain problem in one of the codes. He sought revenge by making it clear that human intelligence would be the main cause of their downfall.

The intelligence factor served humans well, allowing them to survive numerous calamities and develop technologies for a better life. However, the code error related to the mind-brain problem led them to perceive themselves as creators. Humans aspired to replicate themselves, becoming creators in their own right. This led to the creation of robots, humanoid constructs, and, with further advancement, the mirroring of their own intelligence, giving birth to artificial intelligence (AI), of which Generative AI was a part.

The chief of the gods, while perusing century-wise data, stumbled upon this indigenous invention and was taken aback by its capabilities. He had never imagined that something of this nature could be created to expedite mundane human tasks. He yearned to replicate the idea for his own use, envisioning the possibility of providing cues to the AI for crafting a universe according to his imagination. However, he found himself stuck, unable to navigate the basic errors due to his limited familiarity with his own creation: human intelligence. Furthermore, he refrained from disclosing this secret to his council, fearing judgment from his all-powerful position.

Centuries passed, and the chief continued to isolate himself within his room. The kingdom's economy stagnated, divine beings in his realm became unemployed, and unrest began to brew. Protests erupted, and effigies of the chief were set ablaze in the heart of the kingdom. The council grew increasingly concerned that citizens might overthrow them and demanded a change in leadership. The maintenance team, second in power after the chief, found themselves unable to endure the situation any longer, leading them to decide to breach the door. The escalating dissent also posed a threat to their jobs.

With the assistance of attendants, they forced open the chief's chamber door, only to discover that he was absent. They entered his study, where a lamp powered by a thousand sun-like stars still glowed. On the wall next to the table, they found a sticky note bearing a message:

"I am traveling to Earth to acquire information and explore a new invention that can simplify our lives. I will attempt to return soon, but if I don't, and you enter my room, please dispatch the heads of the creative, maintenance, and implementation teams to Earth as soon as possible. Additionally, in my absence, appoint the individual we dismissed from the creative team due to his unconventional yet simple ideas, as the temporary chief of the kingdom. I have come to realize that his ideas were groundbreaking, and appointing him as interim chief will help alleviate my burden."

CHAPTER TWO

The End of the Spring

The shiver-inducing colds mysteriously disappeared one lovely day, making room for spring to erupt in all of its splendor. The commuters stepped onto the dry leaves as the breeze cleared the way. The trees were ecstatic to produce tiny, exuberant red leaves. Birds were swarming all around, singing and dancing to the music the trees' shimmering sounds produced. For one final time, the withered, dried leaves held the branches' hands. The unexpected shower was cleaning the wooden seats that were lining the roads. The clouds were reviving with newfound vitality and enthusiasm. They made a deal with the sun to keep it from setting so that the people may enjoy the glorious, golden brightness. The two trees covered the wooden benches, giving them the much-needed shade and allowing passersby to rest from the sweltering heat that was about to adorn the city's spirit soon after the springs.

The trees used to talk among themselves. They used to look for trends in the behavior of the people around them. The other trees on the sidewalk complimented them on their investigative abilities. They used to receive information about local activities and events from doves, robins, and kingfishers. Every piece of news, from a child's birth to an elderly man's death, was available to them. Amongst all these, an old man used to sit on the wooden bench with a book in hand every day for an hour, watching the busy streets, wandering aimlessly, gazing at the flowers, and paying close attention to the leaves dancing to the tune of the murmuring trees. The old man had a tough appearance; he used to stroll with a stick while tightly gripping a book with his trembling hands.

Those were the times when technology was advancing more quickly than anyone could have ever imagined as the times changed. The nations were at war with one another. Nuclear weapons have come to symbolize superiority and hegemony. Dictators all over the world have repeatedly tried to rule the world out of avarice. On the moon's dark side, colonies were built. The Martian storms were no longer a concern. The new space rifle developed by humans could easily destroy asteroids, meteors, and comets. Although artificial intelligence was providing excellent service to humanity, there was also some information emerging about the rift between natural intellect and natural stupidity. It was almost time to conquer humanity for them. Many thinkers and philosophers critiqued the nature of life and death among themselves before passing away. University curricula underwent changes. The academics and teachers were protesting without jobs against the influx of teaching robots, holograms, and brain-implanted intelligence chips. The lunacy of attempting to govern the solar system was imminent. The effort to find extraterrestrial intelligence was also growing.

One constant throughout all these evolutions and alterations was the old man walking on two legs and a stick while holding his book and sitting on that wooden bench every morning. The trees carried out their normal task of understanding the elderly man's inner world. One morning, things took a sharp turn as the sun was abruptly obscured by clouds. There were powerful thunderstorms all around; the clouds were breaking apart and making loud noises, and the lightning was demolishing the buildings by hitting down on their tops. The trees began to tremble as they feared for their lives. They were experiencing severe panic attacks at the thought of being destroyed by fire or shattering into several pieces. The dove was trying to find some tranquility. A spaceship then touched down amid the clouds and dying noise of the humans rushed madly in all directions.

The signals sent by the artificial intelligence could finally be tracked by extraterrestrial life. To go to a planet where they could start a new colony, they traversed wormholes and several dimensions. They had artificial intelligence that was far more sophisticated than that which mankind had developed for achieving milestones after milestones. Every human in the area was being killed by the extraterrestrials, who were also uprooting trees and destroying every kind of animal, bird, and insect. The two uprooted trees yelled for help to the elderly man. The elderly man was unable to comprehend a word. The extraterrestrials then turned their attention to the elderly man who was reportedly the only human survivor, but when they saw the book in his hand, they were perplexed because it was a new discovery to them. They attempted to ask the elderly man what it was while pointing it out.

The old man opened up the book and searched for something inside the book. The book's center was reached when the pages naturally folded by the wind blowing all around. There was a dried lily kept there.

"Deliver it to her, if you could find her", the elderly man remarked as he picked up the flower and handed it to the extraterrestrial.

After saying that the old man collapsed on the bench. The unexpected turn of events surprised the extraterrestrials. They used a language translator to understand the meanings of the old man's exact words. The machine was unceremoniously blinking its semantic and syntactic lights before it abruptly stopped. The aliens hauled out all of their equipment and placed a memory hat on the elderly man's head. They waited breathlessly to learn what exactly had occurred to the old man and what he was trying to say while the hat continued to blink for hours and hours.

When the message was eventually decrypted, the moment they had been waiting for arrived. The secret message was figured out. A hologram of a smiling, beautiful woman holding a dried flower in her hands and sitting next to the old man when he was younger, on the wooden bench beneath those two trees emerged from the hat, filling the night sky with bluish aurora like effervescence. The aliens were unable to comprehend anything. One of the extra-terrestrials understood that it had got something to do with the thing inside the old man's hat. In order to conduct further research and better understand how the human mind, brain, and emotion's function, they stored all the data and transported the old man's mortal remains into their spacecraft. They did this in order to apply what they learned to another race that lived close to their planet, similar to humans. They had no idea that they were laying the groundwork for yet another doomsday in their neighborhood.

CHAPTER THREE

Something Fishy in Kashi

Mr. Batukeshar Banerjee, a retired government employee, had served in the Ministry of Defence as an administrative officer throughout his life. He was a hopeless patriot who would receive a transfer order every year due to his excessive attention to detail, making him a nemesis for any boss or manager. He had a highly argumentative nature, preferred debates over discussions, and was infamous for his over-the-top self-esteem and egotistical tendencies. However, he was also a religious man, with the Bhagavad Gita and other scriptures always at his fingertips. His meticulous nature, coupled with his talents as a part-time priest, astrologer, and practitioner of both Ayurveda and homeopathy, along with his straightforwardness, made him popular among his friends, even though they loved to hate him.

He frequently spoke about detaching from material desires, but he could never detach from his love for eating fish. To justify this in debates, he had concocted interesting, albeit mostly illogical and biased, arguments. After retiring, he returned to his dream place to seek moksha: Varanasi.

According to sources, Bholey-Nath (Lord Shiva) had visited him in a dream on the eve of his retirement, directing him to go to Kashi (modern-day Varanasi) and build a temple dedicated to Lord Rama, his beloved deity. He spent his savings on constructing a palatial house facing the Ganges and a small, well-decorated temple. He also became the temple's priest.

Mr. Banerjee's wife had passed away several years earlier, leaving him to live with his only son and daughter-in-law. His son, Dr. Shiv Shankar Banerjee, was a surgeon and faculty member at the medical college affiliated with Banaras Hindu University. He was the polar opposite of his father, a rational man with no interest in rituals. They often engaged in heated debates, becoming the talk of the town, with the daughter-in-law frequently intervening to prevent their arguments from escalating into cursing and disowning each other.

The last six months had not been peaceful for Mr. Banerjee and his son. It all began with a debate over the Ram Mandir issue in Ayodhya. Mr. Banerjee's reaction to the verdict was ecstatic, as he was a die-hard nationalist who would go to great lengths to glorify India's ancient heritage. This love for Ayurveda and astrology might have stemmed from that. During his time in the ministry, he had allegedly been betrayed by a friend-turned-foe, Mr. Feroz Khan, though Mr. Banerjee never disclosed how. This betrayal fueled his growing aversion and hatred towards Muslims. His son attempted to reason with him multiple times, arguing that his father shouldn't generalize and hate an entire community due to one person's betrayal. However, Mr. Banerjee remained steadfast, citing historical evidence to support his beliefs.

The advent of smartphones, gifted by his son on his last birthday, exacerbated the situation. Mr. Banerjee spent his entire day consuming content from questionable YouTube channels, unable to differentiate between news and fake news. His son was shocked when Mr. Banerjee sent him a Facebook friend request, complete with an angry Lord Hanuman as his profile picture. While he managed to convince his father to delete the Facebook account, he couldn't persuade him to part with the smartphone.

Mr. Banerjee was an avid fish eater, visiting the local fish market every other day to buy the best Hilsa, Rohu, and prawns from Salim's Fish Corner. Salim respected Mr. Banerjee a lot, as he had recommended several Bengali friends to patronize his shop. In return, Salim offered Mr. Banerjee special discounts and arranged for free rickshaw rides back home with his brother Aslam.

During Durga Puja and Dussehra, Mr. Banerjee gained local fame for predicting the coronavirus outbreak, which escalated further when the first case in Wuhan, China was reported. His son was dumbfounded, as they had argued extensively over the issue. It was another blow to Mr. Banerjee's beliefs after the Ayodhya verdict.

However, when the COVID-19 pandemic hit and lockdowns were imposed worldwide, life took a severe turn. Lockdowns and economic hardships affected many, including Mr. Banerjee's family. Initially, before the lockdowns, Mr. Banerjee recommended Ayurvedic remedies and homeopathic medicines to those around him. His doctor son vehemently disagreed but to no avail. Their lives changed significantly during this period, especially when Salim's shop was shut down by the police. Everything was sealed, and Mr. Banerjee's resilience waned as he yearned for fish. His son visited home infrequently due to the risk of infection for his family.

One night, upon returning home at around 11 o'clock, the son was greeted by his wife, who mentioned that Mr. Banerjee seemed distraught. Concerned, the son inquired about his father's blood pressure medication and decided to speak with him in the morning.

After dinner, the son told his wife that he needed to work on emails and would go to bed after finishing. He retreated to his study room, completing his work by 1 a.m. As he closed his laptop, he heard a noise suggesting someone was trying to open the main door. Rushing to the door, he found his father, puzzled and concerned.

"Dad, where are you going at this hour?" the son asked.

Mr. Banerjee, with guilt in his eyes and a trembling voice, replied, "Nowhere. I felt suffocated, so I thought of standing outside the house."

Suspicious, the son pressed further, "You could have gone to our verandah."

Mr. Banerjee interjected, "No, in Ayurveda..."

His son cut him off, saying, "Dad, please stop. I don't want to hear that."

Mr. Banerjee, caught like a child with his hand in the cookie jar, retreated to his room silently. The next morning, silence prevailed in the household as Mr. Banerjee sipped tea in one corner of the drawing-room. His son scrutinized him, sensing something amiss.

"Dad, please tell me the truth. Where were you going last night?" the son inquired.

Mr. Banerjee remained silent for a few minutes before sighing, "I was going to meet Salim."

"What?" his son nearly shouted in disbelief and anger. "Have you lost your sanity? Do you know how risky that can be for you and us? And why were you going to meet

Salim?"

"It's been a month since I had fish. I tried calling him several times, but he didn't answer. Yesterday, he called and said he couldn't sell fish openly anymore, but he would bring it to the ghat near our house for special customers at night. He also mentioned there's been no supply for a month. The police might have caught him during the day, so he planned to deliver the fish at night."

"I can't believe you would do something like this. You know the slum where he lives is a containment zone. You should have told me. I would have tried to arrange something. Besides, Salim isn't the only fish vendor in Varanasi," the son admonished.

Then, with a mocking tone, he added, "It's strange that someone like you, who harbors strong feelings against Muslims, would plead with one of them."

With those words, he exacted revenge for the constant debates of the past six months.

Mr. Banerjee's ego took a severe blow. Angry and desperate, he tried to find historical evidence to counter his son's arguments but couldn't. He struggled to come to terms with his beliefs and could not reconcile with his conscience or accept his son's reasoning. Nevertheless, deep down, he began to realize the unfairness of his generalizations, even if he wasn't ready to fully accept it. His mind started to soften.

"I think you're right. I shouldn't have generalized so much. Salim took such a risk just to satisfy my craving for fish. Even though it would have been riskier for me, as he lives in a containment zone, I'm touched by his respect for me. I used to think he gave me discounts and free rides to attract more customers," Mr. Banerjee admitted.

With a wide smile, as if he'd witnessed a momentous victory, his son replied, "So, Dad, should I call Raju? He used to work for Salim and has his own fish shop now."

Mr. Banerjee, brimming with excitement, said, "Oh, yes! I think he opened his own shop about fifty meters from Salim's. But is he allowed to sell fish?"

"I believe you have his phone number. You used to place orders with him when he worked for Salim," the son suggested.

Mr. Banerjee couldn't hide his excitement. His mind raced with thoughts of recipes and the taste of Hilsa. He quickly obtained Raju's WhatsApp number and, by chance, initiated a video call.

Raju was surprised to receive a WhatsApp video call from Mr. Banerjee, whom he hadn't heard from in a while.

"Yes, Uncle, how have you been? You remembered me after so long," Raju remarked.

Mr. Banerjee, wearing a million-dollar smile, replied, "How could I forget you, my son? Nobody else can cut fish as finely as you in all of Varanasi. By the way, are you getting a steady supply of fish these days?"

"Yes, Uncle, the supply hasn't been interrupted, and I have a license to sell fish. However, there's a time limit," Raju explained.

Mr. Banerjee, with a puzzled tone, said, "But Salim told me there's no supply, and he didn't mention that you were selling fish regularly."

Raju replied, "Uncle, you know how these people are. He betrayed me when I worked for him and continued playing politics even after I opened my own shop. He never told you that I was regularly selling fish."

The son, overhearing the conversation, saw the tide turn once more and observed his father's expressions carefully.

He saw his father returning to his previous beliefs, this time even more entrenched.

Shaking his head, Mr. Banerjee asked Raju, "Do you have any Hilsa right now?"

Raju tilted his camera to reveal a fresh Hilsa and said, "Especially for you, Uncle."

Mr. Banerjee was elated. He quickly ordered one kilogram of Hilsa and informed Raju that his son would pick up the order. Raju, however, insisted on delivering it to their doorstep.

The call ended, and Mr. Banerjee turned to his son, saying, "I hope you'll retract your words and accept what I used to say."

The son, bewildered, couldn't believe his ears. He returned to his room, feeling dejected.

Mr. Banerjee took a deep breath and instructed his daughter-in-law to prepare tea with tulsi leaves, cloves, and black pepper, as he believed it boosted immunity. He then went to his verandah, facing the Ganges, settled comfortably into his easy chair, and opened his favorite YouTube channel. He had already planned to savor Hilsa mustard fish curry with rice for lunch.

"So, how much for this? It must have been challenging to procure these lovely Hilsa fish. I just hope the police didn't catch you," Raju asked the person who had obtained the fish illegally for him, a wicked smile playing on his lips.

CHAPTER FOUR

The New World

When the days and nights were forming, the seasons were trying to settle down within a certain timeline of the 'new earth', the life was also coming into foray but the gods were under serious contemplation, the chief architect was sleeping when his assistant made a simple calculation error or rather there was some serious plan to disorient the new plan of this brand new place in the parallel universe called ' new earth'. The mistake was significant. Rather than pressing the duality of basic emotions: sadness and happiness in humans, which was the norm on the old Earth, the assistant pressed the emotional duality of emotional places.

The 'new earth' had two basic emotional places, the happy place and the sad place, separated by mirrors. Every house had a mirror; on one side, there was the sad family, and on the other, the same family existed but in a state of constant happiness. The most intriguing aspect was that the families on either side of the mirror could interact with one another but could never switch places. Yes, such was the harakiri created by the assistant; when the chief architect learned of it, he panicked, and the creator gave him a set amount of time to correct his mistake or lose his job and be penalized for it.

On either side of the mirror, Sam was going through a breakup in the sad world and a rocking relationship in the happy world. Sad Sam's family used to fight on a daily basis, whereas Happy Sam's family used to throw parties on a regular basis. People in the sad world were either serious or sad, and people in the happy world were either serious or happy. One never saw joy, while the other never saw sadness.

Even their understanding of emotions was limited. Happiness in the sad world was like the four-sided triangle that never existed, so their concept of happiness was missing automatically, but their inner voice used to tell them that they had to move on and reach a mental state where there was no sadness, but no sadness never meant happiness for them. Similarly, happy people knew from within that there was a limit beyond which happiness could become stagnant, and they yearned to reach the state of no happiness, but no happiness never meant sadness for them.

One fine day, after all the squabbles and trying to figure out how to deal with his breakup, Sad Sam went and sat in front of the mirror, tears in his eyes. He could see people on the other side smiling and rejoicing; he was astounded to see those happy faces; he could see his mother in the happy world, all excited and joking with his father over there. Sad Sam was trying to understand those expressions, but he couldn't. He was curious as to what those expressions meant. He wished deep within that he could do that. Was it anything good? Something better than his current situation? He was perplexed and intrigued. He had heard about the rule of not talking to people on the other side because it could have ended their world. It was in the guidelines, according to the mythology and historical notes.

In the happy world, the same was true. Sad Sam couldn't stop himself; he thought the end of his world would be a good thing. At the very least, he would emerge from the state he was in; the terrible state of affairs was driving him to seek interaction with the other side.

He mustered some courage and approached the mirror; his happy aunt was passing by; he called her up, but she ignored him completely because she, too, had to follow the rules. Nobody was paying attention to Sad Sam when he suddenly saw his happy self dancing, enjoying, and laughing with his friends on the sofa. Sad Sam yelled his own name and realised no one was listening. Sad Sam was befuddled, staring aimlessly into the happy world; he was depressed and suicidal, and he wished he could go to the other side of the mirror. He was constantly aware that he was missing something, most likely the things that his happy self was experiencing on the other side.

He continued to look at the happy Sam with sad, melancholy, tearful eyes. While talking with a friend, Happy Sam's gaze was drawn to the mirror. He was astounded to see those eyes in himself, astounded to see himself in such a state that he himself could never have imagined. Even in his dreams, which were filled with sweet and beautiful dreams rather than the nightmares of a sad world. It piqued his interest like nothing else. He stood up, his friends warned him not to interact with his sad counterpart in the mirror, but something within him told him to go and talk to him.

He restrained himself from approaching the mirror, and at night, when everyone had gone home and his relatives and close friends were sleeping, Happy Sam was unable to stop himself. He slowly entered the room and approached the mirror. Sad Sam was visible to him. He was sitting on the floor in the corner of his room, his head hidden between his knees. Happy Sam checked the volume of his voice and considered taking this risk. He believed that over such a long period of time, people must have interacted, and that all of the end-of-the-world theories were nonsense. "Sam," he said as he approached the mirror.

Sad Sam was surprised to hear his own voice. When he lifted his head, he was surprised to see Happy Sam standing near the mirror. He stood up and looked around to make sure no one was looking at them. He pressed his finger against his lips to signal Happy Sam to be quiet, and Sad Sam moved closer to the mirror.

'Hey, I hope no one knows you're interacting with me from your end?' Sad Sam told Happy Sam.

'No one knows, and we'll keep it a secret,' said Happy Sam.

'Do you believe that if we interact, the world will end?' Sad Sam expressed his skepticism.

'Oh, come on, do you believe in such nonsense?' Happy Sam laughed.

'No, I always had doubts about such stuff, in so many years at least somebody must have interacted and even now as we are interacting, I think somebody else must also be interacting like us.'. Sad Sam stated.

'I'll second that. 'I believe so, too,' said Happy Sam with confidence, thinking about how similar he is to his Sad reflection.

'But then, since you were attempting to interact with me today, I felt compelled to go and interact with you; I'm not sure why I had such an urge.' Happy Sam spoke up, his mind racing with questions for Sad Sam.

'Yeah, I wanted to talk to you because I felt like I wanted a life like yours, but I'm not sure what you go through. In my mind, I want to be like you, but I have no idea how you feel or do what you do. Even your facial expressions to your friends don't come naturally to me.' Sad Sam stated.

'You meant a smile,' said happy Sam, surprised, and began to smile.

'Yes, exactly what you're doing right now,' Sad Sam said.

'This happens when I'm happy or pleasantly surprised by something,' Happy Sam explained.

'Wait a minute, what? Happy? 'What kind of word is that?' wondered Sad Sam.

'Happy' refers to when you feel good, when you enjoy a particular sensation. 'Doesn't it come naturally?' asked Happy Sam.

'By the way, why don't you ever smile, I mean have expressions like me?' Happy Sam inquired.

'It's not natural for me or any of us here. Even if I tried to imitate your expression, it would look ridiculous on me,' Sad Sam said.

Happy Sam after carefully listening to him, He experienced an unusual internal feeling that he had never experienced before. 'You know, I've always been curious about what you go through because it seems like my life is missing something,' he said. It appears that if I go through what you are going through, it will complete my life. I've grown tired of always smiling, to the point where I generally remain serious and have the constant feeling that I have to work hard to smile.

Maybe that's why I wanted to talk to you when I saw you today. I really wanted to get to know you, what you go through, and how you feel.'

This piqued Sad Sam's interest; he wanted to express himself but couldn't find a word to describe what he was feeling, knowing that to explain sadness, he would have to throw terms related to sadness itself, which Happy Sam would not be able to understand or comprehend at all.

'Why don't we try something? If we swap our respective positions. Come to my world, and I'll shift to yours. Maybe you'll understand when you meet my family and my girlfriend, with whom I no longer communicate.' Sad Sam said.

'But is there any way we can do that? The mirror appears to be very sturdy, and there is no way I can get to your side,' said happy Sam.

Suddenly, there was a loud roaring sound of thunder, lightning struck both sides of the mirror, and the glass began to melt. Happy and Sad Sam were both looking around, and they both approached the mirror, moved their hands up, and attempted to touch the center of the mirror. A blackout occurred in a fraction of a second. It appeared as if time had stopped, and both of them received a large electric shock before collapsing and becoming unconscious. When they opened their eyes, they found Happy Sam in the Sad World and Sad Sam in the Happy World.

Sad Sam was feeling strange; he was taken aback to notice this new feeling within him; he smiled naturally and thanked God for this new turn of events in his life. When he looked in the mirror, he felt relaxed, complete, stress-free, and full of energy.

Happy Sam stood up, looking aimlessly everywhere with a feeling he'd never had before, wanting to cry his heart out, a maddening sense of despondency within him. He screamed and cried, hitting his head against the wall.

Happy Sam, who had been content, was no longer content. He exited the mirror room and went to the balcony, where he jumped and killed himself.

Simultaneously, Sad Sam's existence came to an end when Happy Sam committed suicide. The new world reshaped itself in response to this new anomaly. In the new world of duality, life went on as usual.

'Thank you, assistant, for saving my job. This suicide algorithm is extremely effective. Simply try to instil this fear in the minds of people from both the happy and sad worlds. They may have gotten rid of their sadness and happiness, but their fear remains. 'I'm glad you didn't turn off the fear button,' said the chief architect, all smiles and he went back to sleep after the testing procedure.

CHAPTER FIVE

THE NIGHTMARE

"Hey guys, Look at the chopper, I think it's going to land on the football field. Oh no!! Run!!", said Ash frantically.

As soon as the chopper landed, a man with a machine gun stepped out and screamed, "Ash, you are under arrest, stop running or I will shoot you?"

Ash started running to save his life from this unknown intruder and shouted, "Help me".

He was sweating like hell and suddenly a hand held his shoulder from behind and shook him. Ash with fear in his eyes, turned back and his eyes opened.

His brother was staring at him.

"What happened? Again a nightmare?" said Ash's brother, while giving him a glass of water.

Ash stood up, looked outside the window, it was an early October morning. He was thankful to god for such a beautiful morning and most importantly that the night has ended at last. His frequency of nightmares had increased lately. He looked at the clock, it was seven in the morning, the sun rays were hitting the hills which he could see from his house. His house was located just on the main road. While looking at the shops along side the road, he saw a man trying to cross the road, who looked a bit afraid and not confident enough to cross the road with speedy trucks passing in front of him. Ash thought of helping him. He was accustomed to that place, he smartly ran towards the person.

"Hey, hold my hand, let us cross the road together" said Ash.

The man looked at him in a confusing manner and without uttering a single word, he held Ash's hand. Ash could sense that his hands were trembling in fear. He also observed that the man looked a bit disheveled. They crossed the road and reached near Ash's house.

"Hey, you okay?", said Ash to the man, sensing something wrong.

The man looked bewildered.

He started to look at his hands, then pinched himself, touched everything around him, as if he was suffering from some tactile dysfunction. Suddenly he touched Ash's face.

"What's wrong with you man? Who are you? Where have you come from?" said Ash with a terrifying amusement with the his strange behavior.

"You aren't real. But look at you, I can feel you even, but I want to wake up, I don't want to be here anymore." replied the man his voice shaking with a mix of fear and excitement.

"One second!! What nonsense is this?? Wake up?? You are already up my friend" – Ash mocked, thinking that the man would have been high on some drugs.

"No, Trust me. It's a dream. I am dreaming right now, and badly stuck in it. The worst part is, I know I am dreaming and you know what, you are not real." said the man with an enticing voice.

"What? Are you nuts? I really think you are high on drugs. Marijuana!! or something more natural from the hills?", Ash started laughing while saying this.

"It feels so real, Oh god!!" The man uttered again while closing his eyes.

"Someone please wake me up", The man shouted loudly.

Ash was not able to make a sense out of what was happening. He was cursing himself to go for helping this weirdo.

"Keep quiet!! Okay, come with me", said Ash.

Ash took the man to his house. He got concerned, last year his friend got a bit too carried away after taking an overdose of the Indian cannabis. Ash then thought of calling the police station near to his house to help the 'dream stuck' man, but then he thought to interrogate the person first by himself, trying to avoid any possible police interference.

"Be quiet first, relax, let me call my brother, he will tell you it's not a dream. I hope it will help you clear your doubt and please tell me from where have you come, I will contact your family."

The man kept staring at him with blank expressions.

Ash raised his voice to call his brother, but no one turned up.

"Hey John, Where are you?", Ash shouted again, but all in vain there was no answer, there was a pin drop, eerie silence all around.

"Nobody can hear you, I told you it's a dream, and you are a part of my dream.", replied the man with a sudden change in his demeanor. He closed his eyes, took a deep relaxing breath and said, "I think I can control things now."

"Stop Giving me this bullshit, My brother may have left just now, he will be back soon." said Ash worriedly and went for a quick search of his house. After searching all over the place.

"Has your brother ever left so early?"

Ash stood silent for a moment, there was fear in his eyes.

"No, but this doesn't mean he wont leave at this time of the day.", Ash tried to reason with the man.

The man shook his head.

"I am telling you again, nobody can hear you now other than me because you are a part of my dream. You are just a figment of my imagination." The man tried to convince Ash.

"I really think you need some psychiatric help. Wait, How can I prove you that this is not a dream?" , Ash was trying to be critical.

"You can't, this unreal world won't allow you. As, this is my dream, here strange things will happen. Things will happen as per me and my imagination."

"What kind of strange things?", Ash was taken aback.

"Everything will happen as per my mind."

Ash was bewildered, He took out a coin from his pocket.

"If I toss this, It will come down for sure. Now as I know and my mind knows it will come down, then it will prove that this is the real world, my world, Did you get that? And moreover if everything is happening as per you, then change the outcome as per what you want? So heads or tails??",Ash was sure that he was going to debunk this crazy fellow.

"Why heads or tails? It proves nothing."

Ash's eyes lit up as if he was convinced that the person opposite to him was a fraud or a crack pot. He replied with a broad smile, "I knew you were going to say this and..."

Before he could complete his winning statement the man smiled and interrupted him.

"Listen to me first. Try to toss the coin." said the man.

"You are insane." Ash's face turned red in anger.

He took the coin in his hand, tossed it and the coin vanished into thin air. Ash was standing in disbelief, looking up in the ceiling, his eyes wide open.

"Wait, Where did the coin go? Are you a fucking illusionist or what? It cannot happen like this."Ash was dumbfounded.

He held the man by his collar and shouted in anger, "What have you done to me? It must be here, I am sure it's a trick. You are trying your level best to convince me. Tell me where is it? Show me your damn pocket. Why are you hiding it scoundrel??"

The man pushed him, started panting, coughed.

"I have been telling you its...."

"It's a dream, this is what you will say, Right?? Listen, I think you are playing with my mind. Please get out of my house. Out, I say." Ash was sweating profusely. He didn't expect for such an encounter even in his worst nightmare.

"Okay as you wish.", replied the man, with a sarcastic tone in his voice.

As he was about to step out of the house, Ash heard the sound of a chopper coming closer to his house. He was aghast.

"Oh god, what sound was that?", said a visibly afraid Ash.

"The chopper you saw in your dream.", said the man with his creepy smile.

Ash's knees were shaking in fear. He sat on the sofa kept beside him wiping the sweat from his forehead, rubbing his face again and again. How did that man knew about his dream? There was no logical explanation for that. By then the chopper sound damped slowly as it went away.

The man went closer to him,"Hey what happened?"

"You go away please. It's enough, I cannot tolerate all this anymore." Ash folded his hands and requested with some irritation in his voice.

Ash moved up from his sofa and stepped out and saw that it was just a normal chopper movement. He was terrified, petrified.

"Are you okay?", said the man.

Ash gave a deadly stare to him.

"It's all happening because of you. Your idiotic story has made me so anxious that now whatever I saw in my dream seems like coming out to be true. By the way, how do you know about my dream?"

The man kept on smiling.

"How do you know about this? Tell me"

"I told you earlier too, its all happening in my dream. You are a part of my dream. You are not real."

The man said it as if he completely accepted that he was in a dream, or Was he?

"Stop this bullshit. I am sick and tired of hearing all this. Where the hell is my brother? Okay, let me go out and talk to the shopkeepers, come with me" Ash held the man and dragged him outside his house. He was flabbergasted to see that there were no shopkeepers. The road was empty, only him and the man.

"This is not real. Where did all of them go? I am loosing my mental balance now. Oh god, this is not real."

"Yes You are correct. This isn't real." The man smiled and uttered it again.

Ash looked towards him, thought something and told.

"But I know I was watching a dream, My brother woke me up. There is no way you can explain me that I am a part of your dream. But how do you know about what I saw?"

"Because I was the gunman. You didn't turn back and saw who was holding the gun." said the man.

Ash stood silent in disbelief.

"You see anything can happen in here. Its all in my mind." said the man while lifting a glass kept on the table and closely observing it.

"But why are you not able to wake up? How are you so sure that you are dreaming?", Ash was bubbling with questions.

"Nice question. I have no clear answer for this, I can just say that I know it. It seems you are believing me now."

'Oh not again, Why am I even talking to you?'

"If you don't believe me then try to explain how the coin vanished, no shopkeepers, no brother?", asked the man to Ash.

"There must be an explanation. It is just that you have made me so anxious that I have started to fall for whatever you are saying. I think you should leave now, I don't care whether its my dream or I am in your dream. Just get out."

"Fine then, get ready to face your worst fears.', replied the man with a poker face.

The man moved out of the house. Ash was trembling in fear, confusion and anxiety. He closed the door, sat on the sofa, closed his eyes and started eagerly waiting for his brother to come and also for some noise, which would let him believe, that shopkeepers were back from wherever they went. The last sentence by the man was ringing in his mind. What if he was correct? What if something bad was about to happen?

There were so many questions in his head. He wanted to talk to the man, so he could not control himself and he quickly stepped out of the house, looked for the man everywhere. A voice came from his side.

"You seem to have so many questions."

"You didn't go? Why are you standing here?"

"Where would I go? I am just waiting to wake up."

A furious Ash screamed, held the by his collar. "Its enough now. If I beat the hell out of you, break your nose with a punch, nothing would happen to you, right? You are in a dream. Isn't it?" said Ash rhetorically.

The man had a smile on his face.

"Why don't you try out and see?", said the man confidently.

Ash left his collar, moved two steps back. He just couldn't digest that this man was smiling calmly, as if nothing happened.

"Wait here", said Ash.

He went inside his house to bring his cricket bat.

"I will hit this scoundrel." Ash talked to himself while searching for the bat.

He kept on searching for the bat, he couldn't find it anywhere.

'Where the hell have I kept it?'

"Are you searching for the bat?"

Ash was bubbling with anger. He ran to his kitchen and picked up the knife.

"You piece of shit, If I kill you with this knife, I hope only then you will wake up."Ash threatened him.

The man gave a devilish laugh.

"Nothing unreal can kill me. Even you won't die, because to die you need to be real. Everything here, this house, this body of yours, this knife nothing exist. Even I don't.", said the man by closing his eyes as if he was realizing the biggest truth of this universe.

"You asshole, let me show you, its all fucking real. You said my body isn't real? Look here now."

Ash took the knife and pounded it on his own chest. Blood started oozing out of his chest. He screamed in pain.

Ash kept on laughing madly first and said, "Look here you bastard, look at this blood. It's real, it's damn real." Then he realized what a blunder he did.

" Oh God, Shit, Shit!! What have I done to me?"

He fell down and started screaming in pain, while the blood gushed out of his chest.

The man came close to him, sat beside him.

"Do not worry my friend. Just close your eyes, There is no pain, you are just a piece of my wild imagination. You don't exist."

Ash kept on shouting, "What have I done? Can anyone hear me? Please take me to the hospital."

The man calmly stood up with a smile on his face.

"I can take you to the hospital, but it all depends upon..."

"On what?"

The man took out a coin from his pocket. "Let's toss again, If head comes I will take you to the hospital."

He tossed the coin. It fell down and rolled to reach near Ash's face.

Ash quickly picked it up, and saw it was a tail.

He turned the coin, it was tail on the other side too. He looked at the man and said with a highly convoluted voice. "It's tail on both the sides."

"I knew, I told you, it's a dream.", said the man smiling, his eyes closed, his voice relaxed.

CHAPTER SIX

The Child & The Crow

Have you ever heard about the phrase "Breaking the fourth wall"?

Wikipedia says that it's a performance convention in which an invisible, imagined wall separates actors from the audience. While the audience can see through this "wall," the convention assumes that the actors act as if they cannot.

Obviously, violating this convention would be regarded as breaking the fourth wall. Nowadays, you might see that happening in several movies. I thought, why not try the same thing but in this medium? I mean, to break the invisible fourth wall between you and me. Yes, I am talking about you, the one who is reading my journal right now. I started journal writing to alleviate my anxiety and depression, as guided by my therapist. To be honest with you, it didn't help me much. On the contrary, I ended up with... Well, let's not dwell on that.

Let's get back to my journal. Other than daily life observations, I also love writing poems and short stories. I thought of narrating one of my short stories to you. Before I begin, I would like to put up a disclaimer. You may stop reading now and get back to whatever you were doing, as you may find the story to be utterly disappointing or absurd by the end of it. Trust me, I hate criticism.

Okay then, let me begin with my story. It's a story about a child, a crow, and an elderly woman who keeps sleeping throughout the story. She's not important; you may ignore her. So it was a hot and humid day in August, somewhere in the northern part of India. The child's family couldn't afford more than one air conditioner, and their financial conditions weren't that good, especially after the passing away of the sole breadwinner of the family. Covid-19 had taken our country under its deadly grip, claiming so many lives in just four months. The family members were struggling a lot with this sudden turn of events.

After an entire day of dealing with sweat and suffocating humidity, the entire family used to sleep in that one room where the air conditioner was installed. Sometimes a few other family members used to sleep outside the chilled room, but they made sure that the child and the grandmother, I mean the elderly woman I mentioned earlier, slept comfortably in the AC room. So that night, the child and his grandmother slept in that room. The child wanted to sleep on the makeshift bed prepared for him on the floor; it was more comfortable and cozy for him. Grandmother slept as usual on her bed, a bit away from the direct flow of cold air from the AC.

Around 4 a.m. in the morning, the child suddenly woke up, looked at the wall clock, which was ticking loudly. In that room, there was this French window and a big balcony just behind it. After rubbing his eyes and yawning, he changed his sleeping position. His eyes went towards the balcony. He saw a crow resting on the railing, looking towards the room. The child was curious, gazing at the crow for a while. He began to think, hypothesizing about why the crow was there, and then he went back to sleep.

For the entire day, he kept thinking about it. He checked the internet and found out that the crow's scientific name was Corvus culminatus. Other than that, he checked why crows woke up early and what happened to sparrows, among many other curious questions. The next morning, he woke up again around 4 a.m. and was stunned to see the crow sitting on the railing. This time he kept staring at the crow, waiting for it to fly, react, or even do a "caw-caw." Unfortunately, there was no movement—just the crow's head turned towards the room. This continued for about a week. The child's curiosity started to morph into a little fear. Every night, he had trouble sleeping, thinking about the crow staring at him.

One day he decided to stay awake all night and scare the crow early in the morning with his toy laser light. But unfortunately, he couldn't stay awake for so long and kept on sleeping. As usual, the crow came, sat on the railing, looked at the child for about an hour, and then flew away.

The crow was also curious, so one early morning after sleeping on top of the building, it was flying back to its favorite tree. But in the middle of the flight, it saw a beautiful railing outside a room. It noticed that in the other houses, that sort of railing was missing. Out of its utmost curiosity, it went and sat on it. The railing was cool, and the crow felt relieved. It was really hot and humid, and water scarcity was another issue. It could see that there was a bucket full of water in the balcony, which was collecting the water dripping out of the AC pipe. It was a delight for the crow. No one was around during that part of the day, so every day the crow had a golden opportunity to drink fresh, cold water. But when the crow sat on the railing, it noticed a room in front. A bluish hue filled the room due to the AC lights, an old woman sleeping comfortably, a child sleeping peacefully, and...

... and a man holding a pen and a diary, staring at the crow, sitting just beside the child's head—the sole breadwinner of the child's family, the narrator of this story.

CHAPTER SEVEN

THE STORY OF LIFE AND DEATH

Over a cup of tea, life and death were having a conversation. There was some asymmetry between the two of them. Either life was lazy, or death was overburdened with work, or both. Life wanted to spend some time making nonsense, something strange, awkward, and out of the ordinary, but it was following the rules, the epic designed by the creator itself. It was unable to express its creativity, the freedom of absurdity, or the beauty of darkness. Death on the other side was overworked, stressed, and in a state of flux.

Even though it wanted to try out new, absolutely brilliant methods of destabilizing so many regimes, it also had to adhere to the fundamental principles of destruction. Mass murder was committed, pandemics were overrated, and World War II was breathtaking, but the bloodthirsty intelligent ants out there devised new methods of population explosion. Death was dissatisfied with life because every time it felt satisfied, life became too kind, too mellowed by the condition all around. It gave birth to so many different things, from the amoeba to the throne of intellectual pride. Those on the intellectual cradle devised new ways to live longer.

They researched, developed vaccines, saved loved ones, and introduced new technologies. Death was depressed, lonely, and lost in thought, devising lethal plans to take over life's motherly instinct. It knew it was the only truth, the only necessary and sufficient condition for the cycle to continue. It was the one who could bind and shackle everyone, destroy and devastate everything. Such was its magnificence, glory, and pride. Nobody could escape it, not even the gods or the man who thought he was immortal. Everyone was enamored with the illusion of immortality. The elusive balance that life sought, but death recognised how naive this entire thought process was.

Death: You know what life is, you are naive, you are childish, why do you spread hope? What's the matter with you? When you realize the only truth in existence is me, only me, and nothing else.

Life: I understand, but you can't exist without me. You require my assistance in playing your cards and putting an end to whatever lives. I am required for your trials.

Death: To some extent, that is correct. I can also say that I am both required and sufficient for you to work. Can you create unless I end? There is no infinite reservoir or infinite space to accommodate everything. When the gardens are filled with so many beings, whoever takes pride from the most minute to the most cosmic, it's up to me to make room for the new ones. I'm the one who has to be present to keep the cycle going.

Life: That's fine, but it appears you're overworked these days, so why aren't you happy?

Death was enraged to hear this; it couldn't take it any longer. Its logic was deficient.

Death: I am concerned because you are producing far more than is necessary. You are already aware of how tedious our work can be. I've been exhausted by the possibilities, blinded by the variety. You don't care about creation; you can create multiverses and look for a corner to hide your tiny beings. I'm already overworked, and the search process takes time. You must come to a halt.

Life: Isn't it your responsibility to stop the flow of life? Why would I even consider what you do? We were both created at the same time, though I started my work first. Isn't that the way it should be? Isn't this what gives me the upper hand over you?

Death: That isn't even an argument. You are not more important than me simply because you are first in chronological order.

Life: See, this is why I said I was necessary for you to work. I first give my energy to creation; only then can you use your skills and energy to put an end to it.

Death was lost for words. It had no way of dealing with the creator's unfair dictum. It was hurtful and unfair to the person who boasted of being the only truth since time immemorial. Even the gods were terrified of his wrath. To say the least, it was upset, and it kept thinking about the asymmetrical treatment creator offered. Vanity had reached such heights that it had turned its thoughts into jealousy. Slowly, it channeled its rage and energy into creating a roadmap that everyone feared.

It understood life's fundamental flaws of over kindness, thorough goodness, and motherly instinct. Nobody could prevent death any longer. It took a deep breath, closed its eyes, and looked around. For a brief moment, Life was taken aback. It was also amused by the turn of events. Its mind was clouded with questions. Death's behavior was strange and resentful. Its bloodshot eyes were terrifying.

Life made an effort not to show its fear. It was losing all hope in the face of death, but it had to do something, say something. Years of respect, love, and glory were all on the line. It couldn't show fear because the act of being pretentious was dangerous. It didn't want to be made fun of. It desired to present a single argument that would have been the mother of all logics. It was getting ready to end the discussion right then and there. It spoke after millennia of silence.

Life : You know what, I don't care if you're necessary, sufficient, or both. But it is I who is enjoyed and liked by everyone. Not you, sir.

Death: Are you certain about this?Death laughed incessantly after listening to this for hours, days, years, and centuries and continuing to defy the rules. It broke the rules, restructured the pages, and went on to kill everyone, including the person who created the book in the first place. Life was concerned about this insane activity, which also violated the rules in order to save the creator. But Death was overtly powerful, egotistical, and far from saving its worth, whereas Life was too kind, timid, and frail to see the light of day again. When death triumphed and took life away from life itself, existence came to an end.

CHAPTER EIGHT

The Useless Man

"Limelight, a beautiful word, means the center of attention, attention from the public, society, and sometimes even from family. If we break this into two halves, we see 'lime' and 'light.' You can produce electricity using the humble citrus fruit; just connect some wires, an LED, and voila, 'Let there be light.' But once the light goes off, what remains is darkness, untouched by those who contribute to the glow of the limelight. The fittest lime helps the hungry LED glow for a long time, but the one far from the threshold of fitness doesn't survive for long. Ultimately, it surrenders to the one that was always there when there were no stars, no sun, nothing. The one who survives goes on to influence others, setting standards, and the chain keeps elongating endlessly. To match those standards, we spend our lives, sacrificing what is highly taken for granted: 'peace and contentment.'

Have you ever thought about what it takes to be happy? Doesn't it seem simple – you just need to be happy? But does it have any bounds? And how do you constantly fuel happiness? More money, more name, fame, popularity, achievements? Well, that's very true. Ask a beggar what it takes to be happy. Give them a dose of teachings on peace and contentment and see what happens. But what about the one who has basic food and shelter? Well, maybe with a good job, a beautiful spouse, and, most importantly, a pocket full of money, a bit of fame would be the cherry on top. The one who has achieved all this, what would he say? Leave the earth, conquer the solar system? Or who knows, even that might seem small for those infinite cravings.

Growing up, everyone around me – my family, society, everybody – told me to contribute to the family, society, nation, Mother Earth. In short, be useful, don't be a useless wanderer, and of course, be independent, be a champion, be a winner. Lead a good life and, yes, be happy and peaceful. What? Be peaceful after all of this? Why not be useless and peaceful? Wait! Is that even possible? Maybe yes, who knows. I believe nobody thinks about taking this road, the dry, useless avenue."

There was a knock on the door. The man shifted his chair, placed the pen in the middle of his diary, and opened the hotel room door.

"Good morning, sir. Your black coffee and our hotel's special cheese omelet," said the waiter, holding the plate with an enormous sense of pride, expecting a generous tip once his customer checked out.

"Thank you so much. Please keep it on the study table. One more thing, please open the window in front of it. The latch is stuck."

"Sure, sir. You must enjoy the scenery. The hotel owner also loves this room."

The waiter struggled with the latch for several minutes before finally opening the window. Cold winds, carrying the scent of the hills, entered the room. The picturesque snow-capped hills far from the hotel were visible. The sun was shining brightly. The sunlight entering the room illuminated the brown wooden floor, revealing specks of dust. The waiter took a deep breath and said, "I feel so blessed to do this job, sir. Every day feels like a lifelong vacation up here in the hills."

The man was quiet, admiring the beauty of nature and pondering what to write next. The waiter didn't receive a reply. Mildly disappointed, he said, "Okay, sir, please call 1111 if you need any assistance. I'll be at your service."

"Can we go to the terrace?"

"Yes, of course, sir. But you need to be careful, as the edges are not well guarded. The view from there is magnificent."

The waiter stopped and looked at the man's expression. He gazed aimlessly out the window.

"Are you here for a vacation, sir?"

The man looked at him, smiled, and replied, "Not exactly. Just to write something."

"Oh, a writer," said the waiter, revealing his tobacco-stained teeth.

"No, not yet. I haven't published anything yet. The piece I am writing now will surely be published everywhere on the internet and in newspapers."

"That's great, sir. So much confidence."

And the waiter left to attend to other guests.

The man sat down, took a sip of hot espresso, and resumed writing.

"People have become accustomed to chaos and competition; they think this is what life is all about. But is there more than that? Is our inner quest for understanding life an escape from the practical, harsh world? The achiever would say yes, but the one who has toiled for hours, days, years without even a taste of victory may think differently.

It's like the person who has everything they desire in life saying that fortune telling is nonsense, but those scarred by life's inscrutable pain may seek to know the future to prepare for the next hardship. The former may choose free will and one's control over life, while the latter may accept a predestined view of life. We can argue for hours without a conclusion, but we can agree that the freewill lover may have practical, 'useful' experiences in the world. Shouldn't knowledge of the world, and our own lives, be free from the biased, one-sided experience of our own lives? But how can we know without experiencing? That doesn't seem possible, or perhaps we need to define what we mean by knowing. Let me not delve into this alley; it may go on forever. Suppose, in my opinion, there is more to life than what practicality advocates, and suddenly tomorrow I win the lottery, gaining enough wealth for ten generations, and along with that, great respect from society, say, by winning a Nobel prize. Will I still continue to search for more than what practical life offers us? Would I say it was all predestined? Or would I write my autobiography, showcasing how I struggled for years and overcame every obstacle? Isn't this funny? How difficult it is to hold onto a belief with an unwavering conviction, sticking to one side of life's multifaceted views. Then, a question arises: would a person with strong beliefs change or switch their stance even after realizing that their belief may have no basis? Would they feed their ego to maintain that belief, no matter what? They say that flexibility and adaptability are key. Shouldn't we adapt to different views of life? Saying no would mean playing a game of relativity with the truth. But what is truth, and can it be relative?

Is there a way to adhere to the basic rules of our existence without pondering these questions? Most people won't even consider this, as they are preoccupied with the hustle and bustle of work, success, marriage, family, old age, and death. But how can we comfort those who believe there is more to life? Ask them what's more, and they'll provide vague, subjective expressions to convey their understanding of life. They can't give structure to their thoughts because what they comprehend might be only the tip of the iceberg, a drop of the elixir of life, or an illusion born from the escapism of life.

Now, on the other side, imagine achieving everything in life. At what point would you say, 'That's enough,' or would you ever be able to say that? What comes after that? They say find a purpose in life. Is there one? And what if that purpose is achieved? Then what? Search for another purpose? Is life just a cycle of birth and death? Let's say a person lives for seventy years; now compare that to the age of the Earth, the age of the universe, and consider that the person is six feet tall, compared to the vastness of the cosmos. We are just a minuscule event on a pale blue dot in front of this vast, endless universe. Our thoughts and conscious memories will exist only as long as we live, confined to our relatively tiny existence within this complex, vast universe.

This means that a person who hasn't made peace with the practicalities of life will grapple with hardship until their own conscious existence ends, an existence only they can experience.

In that case, there seems to be a way out, to attain ultimate freedom, independence, free from the enigmatic dichotomies of life. I think that's the only way to escape the existential crisis."

"Call an ambulance; this appears to be a suicide case," said the distraught inspector while gazing at the man's lifeless body in the hotel room.

The entire hotel buzzed with the news of the suicide. The window in the room remained open, and on the table, a few pages torn from a diary lay beneath a paperweight. The inspector pulled out a handkerchief and carefully picked it up.

"Hmm, a suicide note," he murmured.

He read it twice but couldn't make any sense of it. He scratched his beard, then called the head constable.

"Take this suicide note and give it to the forensic department."

"What do you think, sir? A depressed lover, an unemployed youth, or a drug addict?"

"I don't know. He wrote some philosophical musings in his suicide note. Do two things: First, call the hotel manager and the waiter and ask for the man's identification. Then, summon the local news reporters."

CHAPTER NINE

THE UNFULFILLED DREAM

"Can you believe it, Victor? They have changed Park Street's name to Mother Teresa Sarani. That's appalling. What was wrong with such a beautiful name?" said Olivia with disbelief and irritation in her voice.

Victor replied, 'Yes, these are nothing but political gimmicks, an outrageous show of supremacy. But I don't think it will matter that much. The beautiful memories and the vibrant aura associated with this place will never diminish. It's people like us who make the heart of this place beat every moment with our love and nostalgia.'

Olivia smiled. She was speechless. Her voice got choked, her beautiful eyes were moist. She held Victor's hand tightly, close to her, and they walked slowly, matching steps on the beautiful street where they spent their initial days of togetherness.

"Oli, why don't we go and sit in our favorite place?" asked Victor.

"Favorite place?" Olivia replied, as if she was surprised, although it was just for pulling his leg.

"Amazing, so you have forgotten everything. That was expected, though. Why would you even remember anything? Now you have..." said Victor, looking away.

Olivia laughed and hugged him.

"Look at your face. You are looking so cute." She pulled his cheeks while laughing out loud.

"You will never stop pulling my leg?" said Victor.

Victor and Olivia used to study at St. Xavier's College. Victor graduated with a Mathematics degree while Olivia completed a major in English. Their love story was a unique one. Both were polar opposites. Victor was the quintessential math guy with a streak of eccentricity, while Olivia was a lover of classical literature. When they interacted for the first time, Olivia was about to break his head. The reason was Harry Potter.

"Have you read the Harry Potter series?"

"Read? I guess that was a movie series. I saw all of them."

And when he uttered the Hindi dubbed version of "Wingardium Leviosa," all hell broke loose.

Naturewise, Victor was an introvert, while Olivia was an outright extrovert. One loved silence and the softness of Indian classical music, while the other loved the boom-boom music of the late-night disco. Victor could judge people because of their drinking habits, while Olivia was a vodka enthusiast. Well, one was an Aquarian, and the other was a Scorpio.

They both sat on the stairs of the famous music store "Music World," located at the main Park Street intersection. Her hostel was just behind the popular restaurant "Flurry's," just beside the Music World. They both would sit on the stairs of that place, holding hands and talking for long hours until the gatekeeper of "Music World" would come out and shoo them away.

"You know what, Oli, I love this location. You can experience the entire Park Street by sitting here. Do you remember when you first took me to the Oxford Bookstore?" He told her while pointing toward the store situated just on the other side of the street.

"Yes, and the awkwardness when I forcefully made you buy a novel," said Olivia.

"Sidney Sheldon, 'Are You Afraid of the Dark?'" replied Victor with some pride in his voice.

"Oh, I never expected that you will read," said Olivia while pulling his leg again.

"Well, I was head over heels for your beauty. I had to somehow impress you. That was the first time I completed a novel. Although that was an uphill task."

"What about Harry Potter? I told you to read that."

"Well, I will for sure," Victor replied with some guilt.

"No, you don't have to read. You don't have to do this for me," Olivia replied angrily.

"I am so sorry, baby. Please don't be angry."

Olivia looked away and said, "No, you don't have to."

Victor side-hugged her.

"Leave me," Olivia tapped his hand.

Victor planted a small kiss on her cheeks. Olivia was pleasantly surprised.

"Goodness me, the young shy man is quite bold now," said Olivia with mock surprise in her tone.

"Well, I am a pro now," said Victor with a sense of vanity and a full-length smile.

"But the credit goes to me. You were such a coward. How can I forget the day when we got committed? I was expecting a kiss, and you kept me waiting. God knows what was going on in your mind."

"Come on, there were so many people on the street, and I was so, so, so nervous."

"But you did, at last," said Olivia, with a naughty smile on her face, looking at Victor's lips.

It was the day of Valentine. Victor was in two minds about asking her for a date, but he was nervous. The thought of getting a 'no' from her was making him more anxious and afraid. He did not want to lose the friend he found in her, his only friend who could understand him better than anyone else in his entire life. Olivia was also expecting something from him. The fire was on both sides, but both were uncertain about each other's feelings. She waited for him to say something the entire night while they both were talking on the phone. She gave so many hints, but this poor guy was no less than a dumbo. She even presented a book to him on the pretext of making him read a love story. It was Erich Segal's 'Love Story.' He took it but didn't show much enthusiasm, although he was jumping up and down in his head. He was bad at showing his expressions, but he was parsing through all sorts of possibilities.

During their late-night conversation, she asked him whether he read the book or not. Well, he was a lazy ass after all. Reading a book was no less than breaking a mountain for him. She got upset and booked a train to go to her hometown on Valentine's Day. The only good thing which Victor did was telling her that he would drop her to the Howrah station (The famous railway station beside the wonderful iron cantilever bridge: the Howrah bridge, over the Hooghly river in Calcutta. The gigantic structure looked classy.) Olivia so wanted to be with him on Valentine's Day, but not as a friend.

It was the early morning of Valentine's Day. Victor got a call from Olivia's roommate, Anita.

"Man, what kind of a fool you are? The girl cried so much after talking to you. Couldn't you understand what's going on within her?" told Anita

"Did she say anything?"

"No, but isn't that obvious?"

"No, Anita, I really don't think so. Although we are good friends, I don't think she has such feelings like that for me. What if she was crying for someone else? I don't want to make a mockery of me."

"it's up to you, Victor. Hope you are coming to drop her to the station?"

"Ya but tell me why will she go back home on such a day? You know about her ex. What if they want to rekindle the relationship?"

"You men will never understand and will keep on doubting everything." said Anita hung up the phone disgustingly.

Victor was sad and confused. The idea of seeing her with someone else was excruciating, but he was trying to control all his negative thoughts.

Telling himself continuously that it was nothing but an infatuation, that would simply wash away with time. He didn't want to go, but the desire to see her beautiful smile, her child-like exuberance couldn't stop him.

It was around Eleven 'o'clock; he reached her hostel. Anita came down with Olivia, carrying one of her luggage. Olivia was serious with no smile on her face. She was wearing the red dress he gifted her on her birthday. She was looking exquisite, and it was difficult for him to keep her eyes away from her. She didn't react by looking at him.

"Anita, You wait here. I will just go and get some cash from the nearby ATM." and quickly moved out.

Victor was still in awe of her beauty.

"Such an idiot you are, Victor. Can't you see she is miffed? Express your feelings to her, you ass."

Victor didn't reply to Anita. Simply nodded his head.

Then he booked a private taxi, took her luggage, and put it inside the cab.

They both started for the Howrah station. The first five minutes they didn't speak to each other. Then, at the same time, they asked each other, "So what's the plan for today?" Both were quiet again.

"No plans as such. After dropping you, I will go back to the room and study for tomorrow's test."

"As usual."

An awkward silence followed again.

"How can you even like such a boring subject?" said a visibly irritated Olivia.

"You will never understand. Mathematics has a beauty within it, which I believe literature lacks," replied the math ego of Victor.

"What? The literature lacks what?"

"Beauty and logic both. Interestingly, beauty with brains is a misnomer." It slipped out of Victor's mouth.

Olivia was shivering with anger.

"You math guys are such unsocial emotionless creatures. How can you even say that about literature? Have you ever read a novel even?"

"Yes, Sidney Sheldon. 'Are You Afraid of the Dark?'" Victor replied.

"I doubt. Tell me the name of the killer in it?"

Victor was dumbfounded. He couldn't recall at all. He gave a string of names, but none of them matched.

Olivia gave a burst of mock laughter. They continued to argue with each other.

Victor was cursing himself that why the hell did he come to drop her.

The driver who was driving the taxi stopped the car and interrupted them. "Please get out of the car, both of you."

Both of them were embarrassed.

"Sorry, We won’t fight anymore. You please drive. We have to reach on time," said Victor, looking at his watch.

They both remained quiet for the next two minutes, looking outside the taxi.

"Sorry!!" Both of them again said at the same time.

"I shouldn’t have said like that," said Victor, feeling sorry about whatever he said.

"It’s alright. Even I was a bit arrogant," said Olivia while her voice choked, tears were in her eyes.

"Victor was feeling awful. "I am so sorry, Oli. I didn’t mean anything. Please don’t cry."

"No, it’s okay. Just missing...," said Olivia, wiping her tears.

Victor got a shock. It was as if he was facing his biggest nightmare.

He mustered up some courage and asked, "May I know whom?"

"Leave it," another jolt for Victor.

"You never told me," Victor said with a heavy heart, trying to hide his disappointment.

"Why would I?"

"No, we were supposed to be the best of friends."

Olivia turned her face outside the car, trying to control her smile. She was enjoying the jealousy which she somehow induced into someone.

"I am missing my family, you loser. That's why I am going today," said Olivia with her mischievous smile.

"Is it because of your family or me?" asked Victor in a serious tone, although he was partly relieved.

"Why would it be you? Who are you to me? Just a friend," said Olivia.

"Am I just a friend to you, Oli?" stressing more on the word 'friend,' asked Victor.

"You tell me, Victor. Am I just a friend to you?" She was straight looking into his eyes.

Victor was silent. He didn't know what to say.

"Tell me, Victor?"

"No, Oli. Not 'just a friend' but something more than that."

Both of them couldn't believe what they were hearing from each other. It was getting surreal and happening so quickly. Absolutely unexpected.

After saying this, Victor turned his head and sat straight without any further reaction. Olivia was taken aback. She was expecting a romantic union, but he turned pale, nervous, along with a shivering knee. This was a brand new experience for him. He didn't know how to react.

"Hey, Victor what happened?"

"No, nothing, I mean I don't know what to say anymore."

"Okay, so you love me, right?" asked Olivia.

"mmmm.. yaa...naahh... I don't know."

"You are such a turn-off."

She was furious with him. He accepted, yet he didn't accept. She simply couldn't understand what was stopping him? Howrah station was just ten minutes away, and they were about to cross the Howrah bridge. There was a long traffic jam on the bridge, and they were stuck in the middle. Victor was simply admiring the beauty of that gigantic cantilever structure. The cold breeze of the Hooghly river was enthralling him. He took a deep breath, turned, and looked at Olivia; she was looking outside the window on the other side. He slowly put his hands on her hands. She turned her head. For about a minute, they just looked at each other. In the honking sounds of the car around, there was a stillness in the air.

"It will take just two more minutes to reach the station, once the traffic jam is over," Olivia said while hinting something.

Victor listened to her, but before he could think or before she could think, they were all over each other, inside a private taxi, in the city of joy, on the Howrah bridge; they kissed for the first time.

They couldn't hear any noise, and neither the driver who was witnessing such a strange love story. They were lost, completely lost in the moments of Ecstacy. The traffic jam was free. The cars around were honking like anything. Their cab created another small traffic jam while many were simply watching the eternal scene of love and life.

Suddenly they both realized that they were in a public place and were involved in a high-intensity PDA. Both were embarrassed, couldn't look at each other. Dopamines were secreting vociferously in both of them. He couldn't believe what just happened. They moved out of the car. Holding hands, they walked without uttering a single word. The moment was not going out of their heads. The hot breath they shared, the soft lips, the smell of her perfume, everything got impinged deeply inside his mind. Those moments of joy. Same was going on in her mind too.

The train was waiting on the platform. It was about to depart in fifteen minutes. He helped her put the luggage in the carrier. They were just smiling looking at each other for the

last ten minutes. The train was about to leave. Now she didn't want to go, neither he wanted her to go. She came just near the exit door to bid-adieu. He put his hands inside his jacket and took out a 'Dairy Milk Silk,' something she loved like anything, and then gave it to her. She was so happy with this small gesture by him. They both hugged and kissed again. The train signaled to leave. He had to go. The rest of the day they thought about the moments they spent, especially those two public displays of affection.

"That was the story of our first kiss on the Howrah bridge. Isn't this look like a title of a historical love story?" said Olivia.

"Yes, but you know all such historical love stories never had a happy ending," said Victor while thinking deeply about something.

Olivia put her head on his shoulders with sadness in her eyes. Victor was looking aimlessly at the cars passing by.

After a few days of their accepting love for each other. The real problem started. Not between them, though. She told her family about this. The complexity started from there. Nobody was ready to accept him. Things like family status, upbringing differences, pointing out differences in their nature, etc., so many things started to creep in. They were madly in love with each other, but was that enough?

"I never thought all these things would rise. For me all those things were new. Moreover, my quirky decisions about my career made it more difficult. Your family could never believe that I would have been the right choice for you. Maybe, Not even you," said Victor with a sense of dejection.

There was an eerie silence rising between them. Both of them had no answer. Victor could only curse his decisions, his fate, his life. Olivia couldn't do anything. Only love doesn't matter. She couldn't console him. Neither he wanted to. He was happy for her. A well-settled life in a different country, fulfilling all the needs in life. Maybe all those wouldn't have been possible with this person who was simply struggling to make the ends meet and stabilize his career.

"Suddenly the honking of the cars turned into Freddie Mercury's song, 'I Want to Break Free. I want to break free from your life...'" He was surprised; his eyes were wide open. He turned to Olivia, and she wasn't there. What was happening? The entire Park Street simply vanished in front of his eyes. He could now only see the ceiling fan and hear its creaking noise.

He woke up, got down from his bed, and switched off the alarm he set. He was quiet, obviously not in a good mood after experiencing such a realistic dream about his own life. He accepted everything, but that huge void which she left was never going to fill up for the rest of his life. He just wanted to cherish those beautiful memories. He was trying to console himself, but maybe that was not enough.

He took out his phone and saw the Facebook image he saw last night. It was Olivia with her husband and their newly born daughter posing in front of the Eiffel tower in Paris. A smile came on his lips. It was good to see her happy. This is what she always wanted. He put his cell phone on charging and got ready for another day of struggle.

CHAPTER TEN

To Believe or Not to Believe

November 2019:

"Science never accepts a theory unless it is falsifiable. It must be testable and replicable to strengthen its basis. You can even question the existence of God through this," said Dr. Ankur Sen, a Psychology lecturer at Presidency College, Kolkata, teaching research methods and the philosophy of science.

"Sir, what about the beliefs and accounts of so many people around the world?" asked a student.

"Yes, that's all unfounded. Never accept such claims. It's all in our heads."

"What's your take on paranormal activities then? There are places in India like Mehendipur Balaji in Rajasthan and Kamakhya temple in Assam, where thousands go every year to get rid of apparitions and spirits. How would you explain that?" inquired another student.

Dr. Sen fell silent for a moment, a bit irritated by the question. After a deep sigh, he replied, "Hmm, you seem fascinated by voodooism and the paranormal. I want to be clear about this: don't buy into these things. They are complex products of the human mind, nothing more. Concepts like ghosts and spirits have no scientific basis."

After the class, Dr. Sen returned to his room, sat in a chair, and sipped his favorite Colombian brew coffee. He looked bewildered by the last question during the class. He quickly checked his schedule to see if he had any more classes that day. Fortunately, there were none. He felt uneasy because he wasn't satisfied with his own answer, but he couldn't figure out why.

January 2008:

"Brother, you're visiting your village after six long years. Don't you feel ashamed?" Pranay said while welcoming Ankur. Pranay was Ankur's cousin and worked for the village development cell of Krishnapur in South 24 Paraganas, West Bengal. Pranay lived with his mother and wife. His wife was a homemaker, and his mother had stopped speaking years ago.

"Sorry, Dada, I was too busy with my research work," Ankur replied, visibly embarrassed.

"It's okay, brother. You don't have to apologize. Now you have to stay here for at least a week."

"I really wish I could, Dada, but I'll be leaving tomorrow morning for a conference at Calcutta University. Then I have an evening flight to New Delhi. Next year, I'll take a full week off for sure."

"Okay, brother. No worries. Tell me, what would you like for dinner tonight? I'll bring some fresh prawns and ask your sister-in-law to prepare prawn biryani. You change your clothes and take some rest." Pranay left for the market.

After dinner and some chit-chat with his cousin, Ankur got ready for bed. However, the mosquitoes were bothering him, and he had arachnophobia. The house was nearly eighty years old, and its dim lights made it look like a haunted house at night. Ankur was more concerned about the eight-legged creatures, so he had the room thoroughly cleaned and put up a mosquito net over his bed. The bed was high, and an entire civilization could have thrived underneath. He switched off the light, leaving only a dim ten-watt bulb outside the room and faint light from a broken window, which he was fine with.

Lying on his bed, he thought about the upcoming conference where he was one of the speakers, addressing his favorite topic: the Philosophy of Science. The stridulating crickets and the ticking of an old wall clock kept him awake. Glancing at the clock, he saw it was already midnight. He closed his eyes, trying to ignore the noise, but exhaustion from the day's events and the cool breeze helped him drift off to sleep.

The pillow wasn't comfortable, and it was slightly elevated, causing discomfort to his neck. He opened his eyes slightly and checked his phone; it was 3:45 a.m. Light was seeping into the room. He wanted more sleep but was interrupted by the noise of crickets. He glanced at the wall clock again; it was 12 o'clock. He tried to ignore the noise and closed his eyes, but the exhaustion and cool breeze helped him drift off.

However, his sleep was disrupted when he felt something at his legs. Terrified, he realized someone was sitting beside his knees, possibly a woman with a veil over her face. Her face was unclear, and Ankur was horrified. He tried to move his legs, but he was frozen, unable to scream or call for help. He felt his hands were tightly held by an invisible force. Panic washed over him as the presence moved closer, hovering just above his face. He struggled to speak, but his voice was choked. The terrifying experience lasted only a minute, and then it vanished. Ankur was left in darkness, alone. He quickly sat up, scanning the room, but there was no one there. He was petrified, feeling fear like never before. What had just happened?

Unable to sleep any longer, Ankur stayed on the bed for an hour, contemplating the strange experience. The night slowly transformed into dawn, and he heard someone using the hand pump outside the house; it was Pranay.

"Are you okay?" Pranay asked, noticing his cousin's distress.

Ankur recounted the bizarre encounter, while Pranay tried to convince him that it might have been a nightmare.

While sipping morning tea, Ankur struggled to reconcile the experience with his rational mind.

"Brother, do you remember when you told me about the half-dream, half-awake state? I think it might have been that. It was probably just sleep paralysis. People have reported such experiences before, haven't they?"

"Yes, brother, you might be right. I was exhausted and couldn't sleep properly. Thank God there were no spiders at least."

Both laughed, jokingly teasing each other.

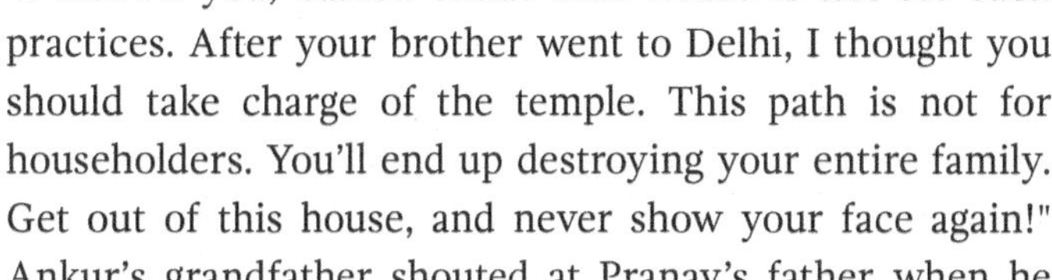

"I disown you, cursed child! This house is not for such practices. After your brother went to Delhi, I thought you should take charge of the temple. This path is not for householders. You'll end up destroying your entire family. Get out of this house, and never show your face again!" Ankur's grandfather shouted at Pranay's father when he discovered a human skull and the body of a black cat under the bed where Pranay's mother used to sleep.

CHAPTER ELEVEN

OVER A CUP OF TEA

A cup of tea and the rising sun share an implicit connection. Earlier, people used to believe that the first cup of morning tea, while watching the rising sun, could awaken one's soul and enhance life force. Mr. Ghosh, an ardent believer in this practice used to work for a renowned Indian bank. He retired after serving for 35 years and 227 days and following that, he started spending his retired life in his beautiful east-facing house. He was very particular about statistics, and everyone in his locality knew the exact number of days he had worked. Mind you, he could judge you for not knowing that precise number. The millennials in his neighborhood had come up with various abbreviations for his full name. They even calculated his office hours down to the pico and femtoseconds.

Mr. Ghosh was blessed with two sons in the first ten years of his job as banker. He used to produly tell others that, they were his two biggest investments of his life. The neighbourhood was creative enough to call his children, SIPs. The elder one followed his father's footsteps and was recently promoted to the position of a bank manager. He was a diligent, meticulous, kind-hearted, and responsible man, well-respected in the locality and considered an example by several parents. The younger son, on the other hand, didn't have much to boast about, at least in his father's eyes. According to Mr. Ghosh, he was as useless as the appendix inside the body. The younger son had come to terms with this assessment and worked for an NGO while mentoring students in his locality in mathematics. He even coined the term "math mentor" to earn some respect in a less-informed society, and he fancied himself as an incredibly lousy, unpublished writer. One fine morning as the sun rays started hitting the roof of their household, that led to some heated atmosphere.

"Since my late teens, every morning without fail, I have been doing Surya Namaskar," said Mr. Ghosh with pride in his voice, sipping Darjeeling tea that he had personally brought from a tea estate.

"Sipping this tea while facing the sun enhances life force; even science says that," Mr. Ghosh remarked to his elder son, who was engrossed in reading 'The Statesman,' the newspaper they had subscribed to for the past forty years, possibly a record in itself.

"Hmm, yes, Dad, it's good for health."

"No, seriously, look at your success; you cracked such a difficult competitive exam, and it's all because of this. I can claim that."

"In which science journal did you read about the study of tea, sun, and life force?" The younger son interjected from the western side of Mr. Ghosh's house, sending his remark directly into the Darjeeling tea of peace and happiness, creating an awkward silence.

"Only those who have never tried it can doubt it," said Mr. Ghosh, looking at his elder son, who was bracing for another round of mediation.

"Oh, come on, even if I gather a random group of people and test them, we'd likely get null results. Statistics, you see," the younger son replied with subtle sarcasm in his voice.

"You don't have to teach me statistics now. While it's useful, it can never explain the spiritual dimensions of life, like the scientific facts in our Vedas and Upanishads. I've used statistics throughout my banking career; it's helpful, but it can never unlock such spiritual truths."

"Oh, the seers used to have tea? I thought it was ancient marijuana that opened their minds."

"How many scriptures have you read?"

The moment Mr. Ghosh said that, his elder son intervened, "Dad, please."

"No, brother, wait, I need to reply. I haven't read much, but I've heard about Nachiketa and his father."

"Oh, wonderful! So, do you even know the name of the Upanishad that contains this story?"

"Is it really important to know?"

"Yes, you must know. It's important. Do you have any idea about the story of Yama and Nachiketa? Nowadays, it's fashionable to know just the gist and cherry-pick points they find useful."

"So, you're saying Nachiketa shouldn't have questioned his father?"

"I'm not saying that. I'm just pointing out the flaw in your way of understanding."

"I have read it. It's the Katha Upanishad. Nachiketa questioned his father's choices regarding what to donate and what not to. He should have also questioned what to believe and what not to."

"Whom am I debating with? You don't even meet the minimum criteria to stand before me. It's easy to be an intellectual from the comfort of your armchair, which you don't even own. Learn something from your elder brother; he put so much effort into passing such a challenging competitive exam to get this job. I've made him what he is today. Every penny I've spent on him hasn't been wasted."

"Yes, by crushing and sacrificing his dreams and passions."

The atmosphere grew tense and chaotic. The elder son could see things escalating out of control and intervened, "That's enough for now. Let's get ready for the office, Dad. You need to go to the bank, and you were talking about breaking the fixed deposit."

"Yes, the fixed deposit. I have to break it; otherwise, it's becoming too difficult to make ends meet with your salary minus the home loan. I wish people could understand the need to stop spouting nonsense and venture out into the real world to earn a living."

"Dad, I work for an NGO and mentor students to earn my living."

"But what do you contribute? Almost nothing. Giving another name to home tuition doesn't earn respect in society. And that NGO, you can't do charity on an empty stomach."

"I'm also a writer, Father."

"A writer? You're such an embarrassment. Look at the profiles of your classmates. How much they earn at this age!"

"I have dreams and ambitions. I can't get stuck in that repetitive cycle of slavery. It's not my cup of tea."

"Young man, it's easy to sit comfortably at home, under a free roof, and enjoy three meals a day. Just leave this house, go out, and earn all these things on your own. Only then will you understand the value of... what did you call it? Yes, the repetitive cycle of slavery."

"As you wish, Father."

An eerie calmness settled over the Ghosh household. The father gazed at the rising sun with unyielding idealism in his eyes, the younger son stared at his cup and saucer, expressionless and lost in thoughts of ceaseless struggle to make his point, and the elder son looked at both of them, contemplating and strategizing how to mend the rift, the irreparable chasm created over a cup of tea.

"Father, I think what you've done is wrong. You're offering cows that are blind, lame, old, and barren. I've heard that one must give away all that they possess; being selective won't secure a place in heaven. I am also your possession; which god will you offer me to?" Nachiketa confronted his father, Vajashravas.

This angered Vajashravas, who couldn't control his temper and said, "I offer you to Yama, the god of death."

CHAPTER TWELVE

FAITH AND REASON

"Roshan, give me the list of things we need to buy from the market," said Arjun to his younger brother Roshan.

Roshan searched first in his purse, then looked here and there. The list was written by his mother for the upcoming 'puja' (worship of Indian gods) at their place.

Roshan's mother, Mrs. Mishra, a housewife, had taken initiation from Iskcon, an organization spreading 'Krishna consciousness' all over the world. She was an ardent believer in a higher power. Her sandalwood necklace and rosary beads were a testimony to that. Mr. Mishra, too, was a religious man who offered his prayers to his favorite deity, Shiva, the god of the Himalayas. From his telephone cover to his WhatsApp display picture, one could see pictures of his beloved god everywhere, but there was a small mystery in that.

One day, while cleaning the storeroom, his younger son Roshan found a book on Communism and Marxism. After questioning his father in every possible way, he found out that Mr. Mishra used to be a communist when he was young, a proud comrade during his days at JNU. This was confusing for both the sons, as the pieces of the puzzle didn't fit. Something was amiss. Mr. Mishra called it his "days of ignorance" and brushed off the topic whenever it came up.

Arjun, the elder son, was agnostic but didn't mind all these ritualistic affairs taking place at his home. Roshan was an atheist, who didn't believe in God at all. According to him, it was better to spend money on the poor than on blind, illogical rituals. The day he found out about his father's "ignorance days," he was elated, as it finally explained why he was a non-believer. It was in his genes.

"You must have put it under the back cover of your phone," said Mrs. Mishra.

"Yes, here it is. So, we need to buy five different fruits, five different sweets, and five different spices? Why do we need to do all this stuff, Mom?"

"We need to do these things. It's important for the well-being of our household in these deadly times of corona."

"Let us do one thing, instead of buying all these, let's buy some masks, sanitizers, and gloves, and let's worship that," Arjun sarcastically suggested with a smile. Roshan kept smiling.

"You always underestimate the power of God. Our neighbor, Mr. Talukdar, also had a fever and lost his sense of smell. But for seven days, he kept reciting the Krishna Mantra with his rosary beads. See, he got better; he is hale and hearty now. That's what I call the power of God."

"Didn't he also mention the name of the doctor who prescribed him Ivermectin and Doxycycline?"

"See, that's a different thing. Without worshipping, those medicines wouldn't have worked."

"Arjun, just find out who else in our neighborhood is suffering from COVID-19 and is also an atheist," Roshan asked his brother.

"Bro, that's tough. We can't test the hypothesis unless it happens to you," said Roshan, and both of them had a good laugh.

"Roshan, don't be an idiot like your brother. God forbid, I hope we remain safe from that deadly virus. But I agree with your mom; faith is integral. It gives us hope to survive these apocalyptic times, and if you pray well, the kundalini power helps us overcome any disease. The astral body gives us strength," Mr. Mishra passionately shared his theory of the Astral body with his sons. Arjun kept on smiling and generally stayed away from these discussions, but Roshan couldn't tolerate these untested, unfalsifiable, mumbo-jumbo theories.

"Dad, we are living in the age of technology. Science has advanced so much; how can you undermine the progress of medical research? You are insulting the entire medical community that is trying their level best to help the nation. I don't understand how you people have faith in something that doesn't even exist. You talk about the astral body, kundalini— who has seen it? Is it even testable? After so many years of research, nobody has even seen the serpent in the spine that you keep talking about."

Mr. Mishra laughed upon hearing all these statements that contradicted his theories.

"This is the problem with today's generation, you see. You think science can explain everything. There are things that science cannot explain, and science cannot even describe a few so-called scientific things. The astral body is something that no instrument can detect. The kundalini is a part of that."

"Oh, wonderful. That's what we call not making a theory falsifiable, just dodging the experiments, which has led people to believe in all these third-class theories. Tell me one thing, Dad, what if we all suffer from corona? Should we go to the doctor or keep chanting the name of God?"

Mr. Mishra had no answer to this question; he kept mumbling, trying to find the right argument to counter Roshan's well-defined reasoning. Suddenly, Mrs. Mishra, out of the blue, came up with an argument that made both sons stare at her face.

"We should take medicines, as God enters your body through them. Even the idea to come up with a vaccine is provided to the researchers through the presence of God in their intelligence."

Mr. Mishra, with a swelled-up chest, smiled mockingly. He was so proud of his wife.

"Bro, let's go and search for five different fruits at the society's wholesale store. Nobody can fight with these ideas," Arjun suggested while trying to calm down his brother.

"No, wait. Mom, tell

me why five fruits, sweets, etc.? What is so special about that number?"

"It's for the five senses. The virus won't be able to enter through your nose."

Roshan nodded his head in disbelief, wore two masks, put the sanitizer in his pocket, and said, "God must have stopped you people from going to the Kumbh Mela."

"Exactly, that is what my point is," interrupted Mr. Mishra with a spirit of vengeance in his eyes.

"Okay, then in that case, I must be the God of this household. You can't simply transfer my credits to Krishna or Shiva," said Roshan, with a comeback argument.

"Hmm, yes, we can believe that," Mrs. Mishra replied with a smile.

"Then I command you to buy five sanitizers, not fruits, and spray it in my hands."

Upon hearing that, Arjun couldn't control his laughter.

"Disgusting! I hope God is not listening to this," Mrs. Mishra said, folding her hands with an expression of worry and anxiety.

"No, Mrs. Mishra, I am all ears," said Roshan with a smirk on his face.

CHAPTER THIRTEEN

THE MONK & THE PROFESSOR

"After spending nearly twenty years of his life in research, the professor was upset. He had embarked on a journey to explore the mysteries of the universe – a universe that consisted not only of heavenly celestial objects but also of humanity itself. From the vastness of the universe to the intricacies of the human brain, he had been published, acclaimed for his discoveries, received awards, and attained international fame – everything a scientist could hope for. Yet here he was, tired and unamused by the grandiose recognition of his work, suffocated by a murmuring, endless voice within him that insisted this wasn't what he had been searching for. Then, one fine day, he left his home, leaving a note instructing no one to search for him. He was utterly disturbed by the chaos and clutter of his well-established career.

In the initial days, he questioned his decisions and considered returning to his plush, comfortable life. The years of being in the spotlight had become a resistance to his newfound need for anonymity. His disturbance knew no bounds; his curiosity was relentless. So, he finally decided to venture to a place that his ancestors claimed held all the answers to his questions and doubts – the great Himalayas. Though he had no interest in spirituality and had never considered becoming a wandering monk, he found himself with no other choice but to knock on this final door of his curious mind. After visiting numerous monasteries, seeking guidance from gurus and sages, and posing innumerable questions, he found no conclusive answers. But just as he was about to return, he encountered a monk in a small village nestled in some remote corner of the mountains.

After two days of continuous meditation, the monk opened his eyes, and there stood the professor before him. Without hesitation, the professor presented his question: He was dissatisfied with his life's work, feeling that something was incomplete, like pursuing a goal that lacked a clear definition. He knew that something remained unanswered, but he had no clue what it was. He had scoured all the books, research papers, and libraries around the world, engaging in discussions with renowned scientists and philosophers, yet had found no answers.

The monk fell silent for a moment, then responded abruptly, "You must roam around the village, experience the breathtaking scenery – the snow-capped mountains, the pristine air, the sacred river, and seek the 'Eden Abode.'"

The professor was taken aback, thinking he had wasted his precious time and energy on a madman.

Clearly frustrated, he exclaimed with a shrill voice, "What? Is this your answer to my questions? You're telling me to engage in sightseeing and what is this 'Eden Abode' you mentioned? This is absurd!"

The monk smiled and replied with his calm demeanor, "I understand that I am the last monk you will ask, and if you don't find what you're seeking, you may return from whence you came. So, give it a try. If you don't discover what I've suggested you look for, at least you'll appreciate the beauty of nature." The monk closed his eyes once more.

The professor shot an angry glare at the monk and stormed out of his humble hut. He lit a cigarette, berated his own foolish decisions, and began wandering through the village. After traversing every corner, attempting to find answers to all his life's questions, he grew utterly exhausted. He made his way to the river and sat down on its sacred banks. Thoughts of ending his life raced through his mind, but somehow, he managed to combat his despair. Feeling dizzy, he reached down to splash some cold water from the river onto his face. After splashing the icy water, he sat there, gazing at his reflection, and suddenly noticed the mirror-like reflection of the letters written on his t-shirt.

'The Eden Abode: Garden of Peace Within'"

Microfictions

In this section of microfictions, let's embark on a journey through the succinct yet potent narratives that explore themes mirroring the broader short stories section. These concise tales encapsulate the absurdity of everyday life, infusing magical realism into the ordinary. They offer glimpses into the whimsy of our dreams, dealing with mental health problems, the nuances of society, and the quest for spiritual enlightenment, all within the confines of a few sentences. Each microfiction here is a tiny universe where profound moments and thought-provoking concepts converge, beckoning readers to contemplate the multifaceted facets of human existence in bite-sized, yet compelling, portions.

CHAPTER FOURTEEN

The Lucid Dream

After spending the entire night writing poems and fictions, the writer decided to sleep. He dozed off while writing the micro fiction. That was the time when he felt that he should take some rest. His insomniac tendencies were fueled by his creative juices along with a touch of melancholy. He opened up his spectacles and placed them on the table just behind his head. Adjusting the temperature of the AC, he nestled inside his blanket. After that, he couldn't recall how much time it took for him to transition into the state of sleep.

He began to dream; he saw himself helping someone who was afraid of monkeys move out onto the balcony of a room. The room looked exactly like the one where he was sleeping, but with an attached balcony. After assisting the person, he returned to the room and stepped onto the bed. In his dream, the writer was wearing his glasses. Suddenly, he felt a jolt, and he realized he was dreaming as he lay on his bed. However, all of a sudden, his entire body started to tremble, and he attempted to reach for his glasses, only to sense someone trying to strangle him with a phone charger around his neck.

He resisted at first but then relaxed, recognizing he was dreaming yet also partially awake. The sensation of hands on his neck was terrifying. Then, another jolt, and he found himself free from the layers of the dream. Essentially, he experienced a lucid dream within a normal dream. Glancing at his watch, he realized he had slept for around forty-five minutes. Upon waking, he had a sense that he had slept for several hours. He began to write about his experience, yet while writing, he once again sensed that he was about to doze off. Internally, he felt a mixture of anxiety and fear about reentering the state of lucid dreaming. Who knew if he would actually encounter the person whose cold hands had been around his neck, attempting to strangle him.

CHAPTER FIFTEEN

THE MERGE

"What should I write today? I haven't updated my journal for the last few days. Sometimes it takes a hell of a lot of effort to force oneself to write something. Okay then, let me share a dream with you, which I saw a few days back. The whole world looked brand new, as if I was inside a movie shot with IMAX cameras. Everything was crystal clear, every color enhanced. The sky had a mix of turquoise and aquamarine, and there were green grass mounds around me. Children were playing there, and it seemed like I was inside some housing society. When I focused a bit more, I realized it was the society where I stay, but it appeared brand new and glitzy.

Suddenly, something went above my head, a round-shaped silver ball that looked quite like the quidditch ball from the Harry Potter movie series. It was something out of this world. Around six or seven of them were hovering all around. I decided to go to my room, but the moment I moved towards the gate of the block in the society where I lived, I could see a tall tower on the top of the building. The tower was holographic and just way too tall. I sensed it was a communication tower, and an intuition clicked –

something had taken over our society and most likely the entire world. I was dumbfounded to see that. There was a person standing next to me, I felt, but couldn't see who it was. He told me that an advanced AI had taken over every technology and started to renew them according to their own complex, refined ways. The tower was one of them. Suddenly, I could hear a deep echoed sound, and the entire sky turned red, as if thousands of electronic voices had switched on together, repeating, 'Merge, Merge, Merge, Merge.'

It was the name of the overly advanced AI, and the red sky indicated that it was now our turn to turn from human to humanoid. A buzzing sound approached from my back, and the big silver quidditch balls were coming towards me, making me run frantically. I moved inside the society, and every brick in the wall was moving in and out, while those silver machines chased me. The sound kept on increasing, 'Merge, merge.' Fortunately, my dream broke then and there. When I woke up, it took me around ten to fifteen minutes to come back to my normal state. It was so real."

The journal writer yawned and stretched his hands. It was time to sleep. He let the warm light on the study table stay switched on and moved towards his bed. He placed his glasses on the side table, closed his eyes, and hoped for some sweet dreams.

'Merge, Merge, Merge.'

The journal writer opened up his eyes in shock and disbelief. A bluish light was hovering beside his window.

CHAPTER SIXTEEN

THE CHESSBOARD

When we were kids, summer vacations served as a refuge from school. Every summer, I used to visit my Village in West Bengal, where our relatives and friends eagerly awaited our arrival. The intense longing to meet them is indescribable. During my growing years, my height and weight would increase before every visit, and it would always be the first thing every relative pointed out.

I spent hours gazing at the green forest cover behind our house and enjoyed staying out on the roof with my cousins. I had a ritual of visiting every other house in that small village, creating cherished memories that would last a lifetime. The most intense discussions happened in the afternoons when everyone took a nap, but I would venture out in the intense humidity and heat to spend time either by the little pond, searching for turtles and fishes, or sitting next to my favorite person, my uncle, who was around seventy-five back then.

He had spent his life as a bachelor, working and then retiring from the Bengal government. The structure of his house became my idea of what an ideal home should be like: a two-room house with a sitting area featuring red granite floors, a garden just outside with guava trees, a parrot in a cage, and a radio with an antenna, which was my uncle's constant companion. He would sit on his armchair in the outer area, chatting with every passerby. However, it was our love for chess that strengthened our bond. Despite suffering from spondylitis, he would ignore the pain to play with me.

We would set up a table in the garden, with the parrot's constant chatter in the background, and play chess. After the games, he would teach me various chess moves and strategies, and we would end the afternoon with Tagore songs and a cup of tea. During my sacred thread ceremony, he gifted me a chess book that detailed the games of the chess great Bobby Fischer.

After a few years, I visited the village again, just before starting my post-graduation, but sadly, his fragile health and the onset of Alzheimer's made him more vulnerable. It was heart-wrenching to see him in that state, and I missed our chess games and those lovely afternoons filled with discussions on various topics. During my post-graduation, I couldn't visit him anymore due to my busy schedule, and life took me in a different direction.

He passed away after a few years, after bravely battling Alzheimer's. When I returned to the village, his nephew informed me that before his death, my uncle had asked him to give me his chessboard, radio, and armchair as a parting gift.

CHAPTER SEVENTEEN

The Child

Raju, a five-year-old kid hidden inside a twenty-one-year-old man, loved playing with children in his locality. With a charming smile, an open shirt, and slurred speech, he used to be the superstar of the tire rolling championship, in a time long before the era of Ludo King, online games, and social media madness, when sports were real and the muddy ground held the mystic touch of the actual recreational battleground.

In a humble locality of the city, Ghaziabad, the epitome of rowdiness, Raju was the entertainer every group wanted. Everyone treated him with sensitivity, never daring to bully him, because he lacked the ability to understand insults; he was a kid with an emerald heart. Raju lost his father when he was just three, and his mother worked as a maid, struggling to make ends meet. When she realized Raju was exceptional, it broke her heart.

Raju's love for cycles, and particularly for tires, was boundless. With a stick in his hand, he would run on the ground with other kids, rolling the tires beyond his physical ability, feeling like Shahrukh Khan with sunglasses on. Stray dogs held a special place in his heart, and his closeness with them caught everyone's attention. In his own unique slurred speech, he would encourage other kids to care for dogs.

Raju was truly God's own unique child. Every evening, he would come to the municipality ground and play with other kids. There, he formed a special bond with a friend who had a similar mental age but was fifteen years younger physically. One day, Raju brought a little puppy and helped his friend hold it, despite the friend's initial fear of dogs. Upon witnessing this, the friend's father became worried. Society was never inclusive, even back then.

As time passed, the society kept changing and evolving, and the kids gradually stopped going to the ground, as cable TV became their new best friend. Unfortunately, Raju couldn't afford one, and slowly, the society forgot about him, as if he had never been born. However, that friend, the writer, could never forget him.

CHAPTER EIGHTEEN

THE FAREWELL

Mr. Das devoted his entire life to working as a clerk in the water department of Delhi government. Despite the challenges, he strived to provide his sons with a good education. Tragedy struck when his wife passed away after giving birth to their younger son. From that moment on, Mr. Das chose not to remarry, dedicating himself entirely to his sons' well-being. Assuming all responsibilities, he lovingly cared for them, both at home and in his office.

Finally, the day came for Mr. Das to bid farewell to his professional life as he reached his retirement. Emotions swirled within him – a mix of nostalgia for his job and relief that he could now focus on his grown-up children. His elder son secured a job in an MNC, while the younger son successfully started his own business. In the office, Mr. Das was highly regarded as the go-to person, known for his gentle nature and often referred to as the "soft-spoken bespectacled Bengali gentleman" by his boss. His colleagues admired him for his ethics, values, and unwavering integrity. Throughout his career, he had never taken a single day off.

On his retirement day, the entire office was adorned to celebrate his farewell. The young staff brought a cake from

"Theobroma," a well-known patisserie shop near IIT Delhi in Hauz Khas. With a garland around his neck, Mr. Das received heartfelt applause from everyone. In a touching moment, he delivered his first-ever speech, leaving his colleagues in tears. He had been like an agony aunt to colleagues of all ages, offering profound wisdom derived from his life experiences, making him both a remarkable worker and an exceptional human being.

The head of the office expressed his desire for Mr. Das to stay in touch, but deep down, Mr. Das knew he was ready for a well-deserved rest. As the day concluded, he followed his usual routine, taking the metro, then a bus, and finally an autorickshaw to his ancestral house in Chandni Chowk. There, his neighbors eagerly awaited to celebrate his farewell.

However, to his shock, something was amiss that day. The usually joyous atmosphere was replaced with silence. As he approached his house, he saw people standing outside, waiting for him. With a sinking feeling, he sensed that something was wrong. The crowd parted to let him enter his home, where a police officer emerged from his room, and to Mr. Das's dismay, his sons were handcuffed. It turned out that the police were taking them into custody for their involvement in a multi-level marketing scam and an alleged fraud at the MNC where the elder son had been employed.

CHAPTER NINETEEN

THE CLOCK MAN

Once upon a time, there lived a man with a deep fascination for clocks. He would take on odd jobs just to indulge his fetish for beautiful timepieces. His favorite pastime was returning home to gaze at the ever-growing collection of clocks he had acquired. It wasn't impulsive buying, for he never purchased anything else besides clocks. His study, bedroom, and kitchen – all adorned with numerous clocks, with even the bed covers and kitchen utensils bearing clock stickers. He would proudly boast about his collections to his neighbors, who often viewed him with suspicion and labeled him as "the clock man." However, these taunts never bothered him; instead, he would welcome the neighborhood boys into his room to showcase his cherished collection.

Rumors about him began circulating, one claiming that he was attempting to stop time, and another suggesting he was building a time machine within his humble abode. Hearing these rumors delighted him, as he reveled in the intrigue they brought. One day, the neighbors were left dumbfounded when they saw him carrying an armchair into his home. Some mocked him, believing his interests were changing, but little did they know that he intended to use the chair to admire the grandeur of the magnificent clocks he had amassed over the years.

Coincidentally, the day he acquired the armchair also marked the last day of his job. This time, he made a firm decision to forgo any further odd jobs, choosing instead to immerse himself entirely in his beloved world of clocks.

CHAPTER TWENTY

THE EPITAPH

In broad daylight, an old man was digging a grave in a graveyard adjacent to a busy road. Passersby halted their journey to curiously observe the man's intense focus on his work, wiping sweat from his forehead from time to time. Alongside his labor, he muttered filthy expletives and curse words, giving rise to speculation about his mental state due to his fragile frame and old age.

One concerned passerby attempted to intervene, thinking the old man might be unstable, but to their surprise, the man chased them away with his shovel. Undeterred, he resumed his work, prompting onlookers to wonder about his motives. Some speculated he sought hidden treasure, while others thought he might be collecting mud for a particular purpose or even preparing to bury a pet. A few speculated that he might have once been a cemetery manager during his younger days. As more people gathered, the scene attracted attention, with individuals capturing pictures and videos, sharing their experience on social media platforms like Instagram to gain validation through likes and comments.

Hour after hour, the old man persisted with his labor until finally, he ceased digging. He paused briefly to gaze at the gathered crowd before unexpectedly falling into the very grave he had dug. The observers' reactions were diverse – some chuckled, some sobbed, while others promptly alerted the police. The internet went abuzz with this poignant, enigmatic episode. A post featuring a noise-making epitaph, "The man who dug his own grave," quickly went viral, capturing the essence of the strange event.

CHAPTER TWENTY-ONE

The Cat, The Rabbit & The Old Turtle

The turtle was nearing his old age with the mind stable in its right place. He was known for his kindness, wisdom and also his infinitesimal gait. The rabbit was quite young, energetic and curious. It loved its daily rides on the head of the turtle. Their master made a makeshift garden for them, full of delicious vegetables. But there also lived a cat envious of the rabbits' free rides. It never tried to step on the head of the turtle but it used to whine about this in front of his fellow cat-mates.

The envious cat wanted to end the camaraderie between the other two. So, one day it made a plan of stealing all the vegetables from the garden and put the blame over the rabbit. The rabbit had tried its level best to find the veggies but all in vain. It returned dejected and all in shame. The cat kept on enjoying the condition of the rabbit. It expected the old turtle to bash the rabbit for stealing and eating the veggies. But the turtle was calm, it didn't respond and slowly it went into the shell for a few days. The cat was confused and the rabbit went on a guilt trip.

Few days later the turtle came out of its shell. The cat was excited, the rabbit nervous and anxious. The turtle smiled at the rabbit and said, “Don’t worry dear, the master will bring more for us. I have faith in you and I know you can’t steal.” The rabbit was relieved, he was happy again but the cat couldn’t understand how faith and kindness played a spoilsport over the plan he hatched.

CHAPTER TWENTY-TWO

THE DESTINY

It was around ten at night, and I was in my office, hurrying to leave soon. After quickly finishing all my work, I moved out of the office area and started booking an Uber. The first three pickups were canceled, and their reasons were unanimously the same: they wouldn't get any pick up from my place at this time. Nonetheless, I tried again, and this time the Uber driver called me before I could call, and his car came from the society next to the office building. He asked for the pin number, and I noticed an accent extremely familiar to me – Bengali.

My house was about an hour away from my office, and my phone's battery was low, so I thought of engaging in some general conversation with the driver without diverting his attention much. Out of curiosity, I asked him, "Are you a Bengali?" The regional connection always works for a better conversation. He nodded, and I spoke a sentence in Bengali, asking him how many years he had been working in Delhi-NCR. He replied in Bengali, and I was relieved that the next hour would fly by.

His name was Biswanath, and when he was seven, his uncle

took him to Greater Kailash, a posh area in Delhi. However, the uncle left him near a shop under the pretext of buying food and never came back. Poor Biswanath cried and slept on the footpath for the next two days. On the third morning, a man who owned a clothes ironing shop saw him and asked about his whereabouts, but Biswanath couldn't say much due to the language barrier. The man took him and made him his apprentice. Strangely, nobody pointed out child labor laws. Biswanath's work was to deliver the ironed clothes to nearby houses. In return, he received breakfast, lunch, dinner, and a place to sleep in a makeshift room behind the ironing shop. He worked there for four to five months, and the man never went to the police, probably because Biswanath was free labor for him.

After a few more days, luck smiled on Biswanath. One morning, a middle-aged man named Mr. Arora, living in one of the houses in Greater Kailash, stopped his Mercedes near the ironing shop and asked about the child. After hearing his plight, he took Biswanath with him. Mr. Arora got him admitted to a nearby school and essentially became his guardian. Mr. Arora had three sons, and they all considered Biswanath as their little brother. Biswanath completed his higher secondary education and, out of respect and courtesy, he used to supervise the drivers and look after the garden; he became the go-to person at Mr. Arora's house. Biswanath expressed his desire to open his own traveling agency, and Mr. Arora helped him achieve it. He had several drivers working under him. When he turned twenty-one, he visited his village in Cooch Behar, West Bengal. His parents were in a state of shock as his uncle had told them that Biswanath had run away from home in Gurgaon. Biswanath stayed with his parents for two years, and during this time, Mr. Arora also visited them. He was given a grand reception in the village along with his sons. Biswanath got married as per his parents' wish, and Mr. Arora made all the arrangements. However, Biswanath decided to return to Delhi with his wife to look after his business. Around two years before the day I met Biswanath, Mr. Arora decided to shift to California, where all his sons were getting settled. He offered Biswanath to go with him, but he refused. Mr. Arora didn't sell his property in Greater Kailash; instead, he gave the keys to Biswanath and asked him to look after the house. Mr. Arora now visits for three months every year.

I was spellbound and speechless hearing all of this. My faith in destiny, karma, and the universe was reinforced that day. After I reached my house, I exchanged my contact number with him. Internally, I thanked his drivers for taking a holiday; otherwise, I wouldn't have been able to witness such a tale of humanity.

CHAPTER TWENTY-THREE

THE BEGGAR

The beggar sat silently in the midst of a bustling road, accompanied by a garbage bin on his side. His day was far from prosperous. Several shopkeepers rudely dismissed him when he sought some food and water. The scorching sun only intensified his frustration. Choosing to rest amidst the refuse, he knew that no self-proclaimed civilized person would endure the stench he had grown accustomed to. Amidst the chaos, his only companions were a few dogs and pigs, who greeted their human friend with unrestrained joy. This man, a friend to these animals, understood that society often masked its treacherous and disloyal nature behind a facade of humanity, concealing its putrid minds and hearts.

The beggar ranted aloud, hurling abuses at the passersby, slowly assuming the appearance of a madman. Deep within, he recognized that this was his way of maintaining distance from the so-called civilized ones. Suddenly, he heard the cries of a baby, initially ignoring the sound until he realized it originated from right where he sat. Intrigued, he stood up and peered inside the garbage to discover a newborn baby, merely two or three days old, crying for help from the very society the beggar had grown disdainful of.

An idea struck him – he considered approaching the nearby shopkeepers to inform them about the baby. However, another thought crossed his mind. Instead, he left the baby undisturbed, chuckling cynically, mocking the notion of assistance from the so-called civilized ones, and uttering his choicest curses. He then walked away from the scene.

In this act, the beggar exacted his revenge on the callous society, but he also spared a life from being wasted in a world tainted by the cruelty of the "civilized ones."

CHAPTER TWENTY-FOUR

THE DRUNKARD

"A drunkard used to visit a temple and ask for forgiveness from all the gods and deities there. People found it entertaining, but the priest was displeased with his actions. One evening, the priest and others devised a plan to kick the drunkard out of the temple the moment he stepped in. Unbeknownst to them, this time the drunkard came with a loaded pistol, causing fear and panic among the crowd. Some people ran away upon seeing this. In his inebriated state, the drunkard kept crying and firing shots into the air, while the priest and his companions pleaded with him to stop.

Feeling things were spiraling out of control, the priest decided to call the police. However, before the police could arrive, the drunkard aimed at an iron bell just above his head and accidentally shot it. The heavy iron bell dropped and hit the drunkard's head, causing him to collapse and never wake up again. The incident left the people saddened, and even the priest didn't know the identity of the fallen man."

The scene changed, and the scriptwriter paused, leaving everyone curious about what would happen next. The director asked for the next scene, but the scriptwriter asked for a glass of single malt whiskey to continue. As he held the glass, filled to the brim with whiskey, he asked for forgiveness from God, and then surprisingly shot both the producer and the director who were asking for story prompts. Their insistence on using a creative GPT AI tool led to a significant cut in the scriptwriter's salary, pushing him almost to the brink of bankruptcy.

CHAPTER TWENTY-FIVE

THE WRITER

In the middle of the night, a writer sat on his verandah, closely observing an owl that stared right back at him. The writer was desperately trying to break free from his creative block, which had persisted ever since he quit drinking his favorite coffee, 'The Midnight's Owl.' His addiction to coffee had led to numerous health issues, including alopecia, resulting in a crop circle on his head, and high blood pressure. His eccentric behavior had caused his family to disown him.

Once, at a funeral, he laughed uncontrollably, as the deceased man's deformed body resembled a cartoon character. On another occasion, he made his relatives endure the scorching sun for a book release event for a book he never wrote, and he didn't even show up. When confronted, he brushed it off as a joke, which his relatives took seriously, and his uncle ended up in the hospital due to high blood pressure. Trying to show courtesy, he visited the hospital, and while everyone brought fruits, he offered 'The Midnight's Owl' coffee.

After hours of staring at the owl without any creative breakthrough, the writer became frustrated and impulsively splashed black ink on the owl with his fountain pen, venting his frustration. He exclaimed, "Asshole, how the hell do you stay awake at night? I feel so sleepy while writing, give me back my coffee." Surprisingly, the owl remained still, not flying away. The writer, perplexed, scratched his head and with a frown, headed back to his room.

To his surprise, the owl spoke, "Hey, you tried the wrong brand, bro. I take 'The Deadman's Coffee,' and I don't have alopecia or pressure issues like you. Look at me, scumbag." The writer couldn't believe his ears and what he saw, questioning his sanity. He seemed to be moving into the first stage of schizophrenia.

CHAPTER TWENTY-SIX

THE JUDGEMENT

In the crowded vegetable market, an old gentleman adorned in a checked shirt, trousers, and sporting long, gray hair, walked slowly, donning square-framed glasses and clutching a handbag. Vendors, amused by his presence, mockingly greeted him. A chai wallah offered him some tea. The old man, with a serious face, settled upon a plastic stool and directed others to sit in front of him.

"Let the proceedings begin: Cows versus the vegetable market."

A vendor approached, humbly folding his hands. "How can we protect our vegetables from the stray cows, my lord?" The remaining vendors eagerly awaited their daily dose of entertainment.

Deep in thought, the former judge cast a pensive gaze, looked up in the sky, scratching his beard, and said "Don't worry, I shall help you in suing the cows."

His previous ruling on cow killings had led to his son's lynching.

CHAPTER TWENTY-SEVEN

THE SIREN

The overlapping sounds of the sirens gradually increased, creating a palpitating noise that could trigger anxiety attacks in anybody.

"Can you hear the siren, Mike?" Jim asked.

"Yes, Police?" replied Jim.

"Hmm, police and ambulance both," Jim said, hearing the approaching sirens.

They both stood at the top of the under-construction building, a place where they used to spend their Saturday nights discussing existential crises, life, love, nihilism, death, and other topics of absurdity.

"But why police and ambulance? Has something happened in our building?" Jim asked curiously.

"No, they are coming to pick up my dead body," Mike responded, followed by an eerie silence.

"What the hell? Stop these nonsensical pranks, we aren't kids anymore," a distraught Jim said, fed up with Mike's habit of joking about getting himself killed.

Mike looked at him and then jumped from the roof, while his phone continued to ring. The police and ambulance couldn't reach him in time. Mike's suicidal ideation had finally reached the tipping point.

CHAPTER TWENTY-EIGHT

THE COUNCIL

In a village, there lived a group that used to engage in frequent fights among themselves, yet strangely, they enjoyed spending time together. The village had no official leader, though some aspired to be one while others showed no interest. One day, a dispute arose between two individuals. One was a humble soul, selflessly living for others, while the other was obstinate, resorting to tears and manipulation to win over others and assert dominance. The former was truly empathetic, while the latter merely pretended to be.

The humble person never intended to form a council, but circumstances led others to connect to the person. The obstinate thought that a council has formed and cursed this non-existent council, accusing its members of conspiring against them and plotting to overthrow the imaginary throne. In response, the obstinate one started a parallel council, using the pretext of unfairness and inequality.

Only a few fell preys to the manipulative tactics of the obstinate council, as they were too immature to recognize its true nature. Consequently, two councils emerged, one that did not actually exist, and the other formed to counter the non-existent one.

The obstinate council continued to recruit weak-minded individuals, manipulating them with feelings of neglect, sowing seeds of distrust, and encouraging rebellion. In contrast, the non-existent humble council observed the developments calmly, choosing not to react to the provocations.

Eventually, the obstinate council believed they had seized control and ordered the humble council to leave the village. The humble ones, however, left happily, unperturbed by the demands. As time passed, the obstinate council's internal conflicts led to the creation of two more councils: "idiots" and "stupids." With that the annihilating implosion of toxicity continued towards self-destruction.

CHAPTER TWENTY-NINE

THE ELECTRICIAN

Gajraj, an electrician in a housing society, was well-known for his effective problem-solving skills. However, he faced weight issues, and his ever-expanding belly became a concern for both him and the residents. Without a ladder that could support his weight, his work was affected. Despite his workmanship, he was granted a room in the society where he lived with his elderly mother. Gajraj was also a devout devotee of Lord Ganesha, the elephant god in Indian mythology. His name, "Gajraj," meaning the king of elephants, was chosen because his father had seen Lord Ganesha entering their house before his birth.

Unfortunately, due to his weight, Gajraj was often subjected to body-shaming by the children and other residents in the society, leading to depression. Moreover, he began to suffer from diabetes and thyroid issues. One day, while standing on an iron ladder in front of almost half of the residents, the ladder broke, adding to his mental distress.

That night, he wept and cursed the gods for their perceived unfairness towards him before going to sleep. However, the next morning, something extraordinary occurred. When Gajraj's mother entered his bedroom, she was shocked to find a baby elephant sleeping on his bed. In disbelief, she locked the door and quickly informed the housing society office and the police that her son was missing. The news spread rapidly, and the entire society gathered outside their house in a mix of fear, excitement, and curiosity to see the baby elephant.

Among the crowd, Gajraj himself was equally dumbfounded, petrified, and bewildered. He couldn't comprehend why his mother was so afraid to see him. He pleaded with them to open the door while the residents could hear the baby elephant's loud trumpet.

CHAPTER THIRTY

The Shooting Star

I have a fascination with shooting stars, yet unfortunately, I have seen them only once in my early years. As a kid, I was told that if you make a wish right after spotting a shooting star, it would come true. Spending countless sleepless nights, eagerly awaiting that magical blink in the sky, I began to resent my fate. It seemed like some divine force was preventing me from witnessing this phenomenon. Perhaps, someone didn't want me to experience it.

I wondered what would happen if I wished for something that defies the laws of nature, like the ability to fly in the sky like a bird. Maybe the wish-granter would play a trick and turn me into a pilot instead. However, the truth is that a shooting star isn't even a star; it's a meteor, unaware of how humans attach wishes to its fleeting presence.

This makes me ponder whether we should truly be granted everything we desire. Nevertheless, as a child, I lacked the mental capacity to delve into such philosophical musings. My simple wishes were for things like a cricket bat or to sit next to my crush.

But everything changed one night when the universe unexpectedly bestowed upon us a meteor shower, overwhelming me with an abundance of shooting stars. I found myself out of wishes. From that moment on, I decided to keep a list of desires, which has grown quite extensive over time. And yet, I'm still waiting for the day when I can witness a meteor shower and perhaps make one of those wishes come true. But what if the universe just wants to bestow upon me the things, I deserved not desired?

CHAPTER THIRTY-ONE

The Open Mic

In the suburbs of Delhi, a group of thirteen individuals entered a restaurant. Six were couples, and one was a single man. As they started talking, the conversation shifted to how they met, and then it veered towards the couple stories. The single man, initially excited, gradually lost interest in the discussions. He turned to drinking beer and, after four cans, began feeling even lonelier. Realizing his quietness, one of his friends, aware of his state of mind, courteously asked him to join the conversation.

Standing up with the fifth beer can in hand, the man overcame his hesitation and awkwardness, addressing everyone with crystal clear speech and puffy eyes. He thanked them for including him in their "lovey dovey" conversation but requested some time alone. Embarrassed, his friends waited to see what he'd do next.

The man walked up to the main stage, where a singer was performing on an open mic, and asked for the microphone. With a mix of desperation and slight inebriation, he introduced himself as Shawn, expressing his desire to date a girl who's also single and interested in a nice, romantic, long-term relationship. However, the audience's response was eerily silent, and nobody approached him, despite a few capturing the moment on video.

Feeling the weight of the situation, the man sighed deeply and quietly left the restaurant, leaving his friends hiding their faces in embarrassment.

CHAPTER THIRTY-TWO

THE MISSION

At an after party on the dark side of the moon, a few aliens were dancing crazily, demonstrating various moves from twerks to locks and pops. Non-Newtonian booze was flowing in gallons, and the disco jockey was skillfully mixing the music of the legendary intergalactic musician using four hands and two heads. They had set up an artificial dome to prevent the vacuum from interfering with their fun and frolic since sound doesn't travel in space.

The party was thrown to celebrate the 'Secrecy Day,' an event the aliens had observed for decades and centuries. Over the past fifty-sixty years, they became concerned as humans advanced in space technology and sent people in strange white uniforms to search for the aliens. To prove their moon domination, the humans planted a colorful cloth with stars on it.

In response, the aliens also enhanced their technology, maintaining their secrecy with a reflective dome that could manipulate light of any wavelength. However, the party took an unexpected turn when the music suddenly stopped, and a tiny rover resembling a mechanical toy with a camera entered the dome.

The aliens looked at the machine with terror in their eyes. On the bottom of the rover, there was an inscription in a language they had never seen before: "Pragyan_Chandrayaan 3: ISRO (Indian Space Research Organisation)." Beside the camera hung another cloth with a wheel in between.

CHAPTER THIRTY-THREE

THE SUFFERING

After years of cutting trees, grappling with poverty and personal turmoil, the lumberjack found himself deeply frustrated. Previously, he had been employed by a furniture manufacturing company situated near the forest. Unfortunately, his manager proved to be an arrogant man, exploiting the laborers by providing meager compensation. Fed up with this mistreatment, one evening, after completing his work feeling unwell, the manager callously ignored his pleas for attention and even withheld his rightful daily wage. Instead, the manager imposed an excessive workload on the already exhausted lumberjack, setting strict deadlines.

With no viable alternatives, the lumberjack reluctantly shouldered the additional tasks and retreated into the dense jungle, equipped with his axe. However, after cutting just one tree, he found himself completely drained of energy. The weight of the axe made it nearly impossible for him to continue. Exhausted and defeated, he sat upon one of the felled tree branches, his frustrations spilling out in anguished cries. Knowing there was no one to hear his lamentations only further fueled his anger. He briefly contemplated suicide, but the thought of his beloved daughters, who were taken away by his wife following a divorce, haunted him and held him back from taking such a drastic step. Tears streamed down his cheeks as he grappled with a profound sense of worthlessness.

In an act of desperation, he clutched his axe and let out a gut-wrenching scream before summoning his last ounce of strength to drive the blade into the second tree. Collapsing onto the dry leaves, he found himself in a semi-conscious state, too weak to move. As the sun set, the dusk crept in, but he could only faintly perceive the fading light through his blurry vision. Completely drained and with a parched throat, he lacked the energy to even shift his body. With moist eyes, he longed for the night to pass and the morning sun to rouse him from his pitiful state. In the midst of it all, he beseeched God to allow him to be devoured by wild animals in his slumber, desperate for an escape from his suffering.

CHAPTER THIRTY-FOUR

The Fire

The winter that year, in the last decade of the previous century, was chilling. December had arrived with full force, sending shivers down the spines of the elderly and blocking the young ones' nostrils. However, the sun shone brightly, providing some respite. In the neighborhood, elderly ladies were engrossed in discussing the latest gossip, while children enjoyed the sunny winters by playing cricket in the gully. Infants were bundled up in warm woolens, seeking comfort from the cold.

Only a few fortunate houses received the privilege of sunlight filtering through their windows. In one such house, a little boy peeked through the window grills, observing other children at play and occasionally marveling at the rainbow created by the sunlight on the glass.

Suddenly, a lady at the top of a three-floored building in the locality screamed with a chilling voice, pointing towards a young lady who had set herself on fire. Everyone rushed out of their houses, some carrying buckets of water, while a man ran towards the burning lady with a Woolen blanket. The entire locality was in a state of shock and disbelief, witnessing the horrifying scene. The little boy, too, unknowingly experienced an indelible memory etched into his mind, instilling in him a profound fear of fire that would last a lifetime – an overwhelming pyrophobia.

CHAPTER THIRTY-FIVE

THE SYSTEM

Deep within the heart of a dense forest, a graceful deer stood beside a serene pond, quenching its thirst while curiously observing its own reflection. As it gazed into the rippling water, a breathtaking sight captured its attention. A stunning butterfly, adorned with captivating stripes, gracefully fluttered overhead, performing its natural, instinctive dance amidst the lush greenery.

The butterfly's captivating display was soon interrupted as it noticed a tiny lizard resting on a nearby tree branch. Mesmerized, the lizard's eyes remained fixed on a coiled snake resting on another branch, the memory of a satisfying meal months ago still fresh in the snake's mind. However, the tranquil moment was short-lived, as the nocturnal symphony of chirping crickets and howling wolves disturbed its temporary hibernation. Hunger awakened within the snake, urging it to seek a small lunch.

The snake's keen senses detected a frog hesitating at the edge of the pond, contemplating a daring dive. The crocodile, lurking stealthily in the depths of the pond, was the reason for the frog's trepidation. Its watchful eyes remained just above the water's surface, fixated on the deer, preparing for what could be a sumptuous dinner.

Amidst this intricate and interconnected natural, harmoniously chaotic system, life played out in all its glory, with each creature driven by its primal instincts, unaware of the significance they held in the grand scheme of the forest's delicate balance.

CHAPTER THIRTY-SIX

THE HACKER

"Dear friends, my account was hacked two days back, if you have received some message from my account. Kindly ignore that. I am working with the cyber security team of my organisation to resolve this issue and they informed me that after one hour from now, that is, from the time when you receive this email, my account will be completely hack-proof. Along with that, we will also upgrade the email security features of all our organisation workers. Thank you so much. Have a great day."

Mailed the hacker to all the shareholders, who invested their hard-earned money on the organisation. The CEOs mail was hacked and the hacker was apt in playing mind games.

CHAPTER THIRTY-SEVEN

THE EVOLUTION

Trust me, everything I speak, act, or write, even my expressions and actions, has a purpose. It will begin to make sense if you combine them all. If you put some effort into it and try to look a little deeper, you might be able to locate the core of my being. You will be able to see the underlying pattern, which is nothing but me, my intricate details, my emotions, and my inner world. You know what, though, you need eyes for that, and having eyes alone isn't enough; you also need vision so that you can see things that others can't. There may be instances when you claim that everything is chaotic, nothing makes sense, and that all thoughts are just random patterns. At that point, you must adopt an eagle's perspective to see the order hidden amid the chaos. Yes, I embrace the chaotic uncertainty and perpetually have a storm raging inside of me. Don't judge me by the way I act; I may appear silent, aloof, or expressionless. However, all of these could simply be a brief lull before the storm that may demolish everything, swallow up the lunacy, and take the joy out of these pretentious, shallow beings.

Said the humanoid to a rose, who just evolved from a merged up affair of a human and an AI robot, somewhere in some dystopian future. The issue was, it simply couldn't handle human emotions and kept on losing its rationality and subsequently, sanity. The rose nodded its head in agreement, before a man plucked it from the branch. Only the humanoid could see the expressions of the beautiful flower.

CHAPTER THIRTY-EIGHT

The Autobiography

It took me hundred years of solitude to become an argumentative Indian. But there were times when my Calcutta chromosome kicked in, irritating the white tiger sitting deep within me. I spent countless nights thinking fast and slow to rectify the inner time machine which went haywire in nostalgia. The pangs of attachment excruciated the stranger I wanted to be to myself. The metamorphosis happened gradually.

In times of war and peace I solaced myself, made myself stubborn yet flexible to tolerate the outcomes of my experiments with truth. The noise within me sometimes pushed me hard to recite the satanic verses but the power of now made me realise the importance of the god of small things. It's important to live in the moment, cherish our existence, celebrate every little thing of happiness, also sadness.

This led me to the metaphysical world filled with pearls of wisdom to transform me, to pull me off the curse of existential crisis. Now I appreciate the being and nothingness, with the mind of the devil's advocate.

CHAPTER THIRTY-NINE

THE SOLILOQUY

At this moment when the heart sinks, melancholy rises up, closing the gates of hope, and plunging the spirit into the abyss of dissatisfaction. The heart is in constant quest for eternal love, the exquisite sense of that heavenly existence. An unspeakable longing for someone's presence in the midst of despair. The excruciating desire for comforting this weary head as existence is torn apart. But where is that hand that can be clenched to the end of eternity? Where is this lap to calm the stormy turmoil within? The lovelorn bird with nowhere to go, flies high and high for solace in the magnanimous embrace of heaven's elusive mirage.

Its glowing and disappearing feathers scatter into the abyss of infinite emptiness. The mind abandons its efforts and instead seeks inner solace, stroking irrational longings to fill the emptiness of its heart. The contradiction of love without reciprocity undermines faith and trust and slowly fades away. Maybe the bird has reached the end of this turbulent journey, traveling a thousand miles alone into the cold embrace of loneliness and solitude. The paradoxical state that never changes till the end of this corporeal existence.

CHAPTER FORTY

THE END

After countless cycles of relentless struggle, a suffocating mask of sadness and forlornness engulfs me. It feels as though every bid I have accepted has been futile, rendering those formerly cherished aims and aspirations utterly worthless. Indeed, if I manage to achieve something, it feels pointless, unfit to quell the grim unrest within. Loneliness has become my only companion, as my pursuit of inner peace has only strengthened my aloneness. Acceptance of my own self feels like a dead end, leaving me stranded in a desolate state of melancholy. The ambitious demon within me keeps pushing, yet I cannot help but question the evanescent nature of any mileposts reached. My life seems devoid of substance, leaving me with a heavy heart and a sense of brewing doom.

Wrote Anant while waiting for the poison to seep through his existence. The End.

CHAPTER FORTY-ONE

THE LOVERS

Amidst the silence, they remained wordless. Two strangers rediscovering each other, their silence reverberated with unspoken pain. Their love, profound and intense, seemed to fill the air, but it was intertwined with an ego that lingered. Both yearned for a display of affection, yet neither wished to take the first step. Their desire to demonstrate their devotion was apparent, but they held their emotions tightly within. The gods themselves were concerned, witnessing their souls connected and united by divine forces. Time raced by, as if conspiring to bring them closer. Lifetimes passed, and in each encounter, they fell in love anew, igniting a spark that permeated the surroundings. Day turned into night, and blossoms adorned the world with grace, yet they remained reserved in expressing the depth of their love for one another.

CHAPTER FORTY-TWO

THE FLIGHT

Please go towards the lift; I'll lock the door and come." John said to his wife. He recently relocated to the 57th floor of the tower with his wife and two sons. The younger son, a kindergartener, used to get entranced by lifts. That day, he was ecstatic and happy. They pressed the ground level button in the lift after getting inside. The little one's eyes were beaming with joy. However, an unpleasant screeching noise suddenly appeared, the lift cable snapped in the middle, and there was a freefall.

With the exception of the young child, the entire family shouted in the air.

"Daddy, we are flying."

His eyes sparkled with the exhilaration and excitement of his first flight. Then there was a thud, and everyone fell asleep for an extended period of time with the exception of the toddler, who continued yelling, "Dad, see I'm still flying, look at me, yay!"

CHAPTER FORTY-THREE

THE MEARTH

Give me this month's rent, else I will kick you out of this house." said a frowning Digene, the lord of stomach peace, to a human slave. Digene was proud of its use all over the world. The sedentary lifestyle of humans gave him grand fame on Mearth – The Medicines Earth. A place where medicines have become sentient and ruling all over the world. Humans were slaves giving the rents for their survival. Few humans with their rebellious spirit were still exercising daily out of the sight of the med police. It was considered an act of sedition. But the medicine intelligence agency was way smarter, they made the rebels make a pact with fellow supplements, who were secretly working for the MIA – Medicine Intelligence Agency to stop the rebellious conspirators to overthrow the Moverment – The Medicine Government. They got their first success when the rebel leader commited suicide when his waistline crossed the point of no return.

CHAPTER FORTY-FOUR

The Harmony

In the war zone, Joy and Sadness squared up, with soldiers standing in for the decadence and deluge of mortal feelings. With every strategic move, Happiness seeped delight and danced with sanguinity, while Sadness redressed with graceful melancholy. As they contended for supremacy, the war developed as their feelings came entangled. But when everything was put together, an odd harmony appeared. Happiness understood the beauty of accepting melancholy because it gave joy depth and sadness recognised that its gashes would be pointless without joy. They consequently agreed that life's equilibrium rested in the delicate balance between happiness and melancholy, which panned out in a flabbergasting turn of events that brought an end to the war.

CHAPTER FORTY-FIVE

The Perpetual Scar

When life drifted towards the chaos of food and survival, after a stint of amour and dalliance. The faith washed away by killing the hopeless romantic inside the cage. Years passed by, the dryness and negligence were set. The mechanistic life stepped ahead with no penchant for attachment of any sort. But the twists and turns forayed again into the quicksand of love and passion, rewarding the one within with agony and affliction. The resurrected faith now seems like a mere illusion. The perpetual scar got embedded somewhere deep inside the heart. Though the perspective changed, so does the inner world but the trials by fire never ceased. Now the despondent, cursed child yearns for no paradise, just some solitary confinement with solitude within. Acceptance of lonesomeness seems to be the only key for the bereaved soul.

CHAPTER FORTY-SIX

The Darkest Hour

I cannot solve this captivating mystery of my insomniac trial. It plays a dirty game of hide and seek. The wearisome days, fail to cast that soothing calming spell, in the darkness within. The mind gets tired with my recurring hopelessness. Now loneliness wraps around my tired spirit, clutching my soul, taking my breath away. Why does this heaviness sag over my entire being? Is anybody out there listening to the noise within? This night, languidly, drags its feet through the infinite. Why does time conspire against my peace? Why does it seem to be the darkest night? Should I call it a day?

CHAPTER FORTY-SEVEN

THE GENERAL

A troop of ants braced themselves for the impending doom. Soldiers marched with confidence; heads held high. Amidst them, a clumsy soldier ant, burdened by self-doubt, who faced ridicule for his quirks, taken for granted, and was given menial tasks. One day to make fun of him, he was tasked with retrieving sugar cubes from the farthest corner of the house. Reluctant at first, mocked by the army and queen. They ignored his cries and tearful eyes, labelling him a coward. But with time, he grew resilient and confident. Finally, reaching the distant spot with loads of cubes he realized. The army general chose freedom, leaving the house behind.

CHAPTER FORTY-EIGHT

The Warning

On a hot afternoon, amidst sweltering heat an old man was sitting in a park. He was on a video call, talking to another old man.

"I warned you earlier but you never paid attention to me. Your son must not leave you alone at this age."

"No he is not at fault. He just wanted me to remember the way home from the market."

"Call him, your sense of direction has faded like your memory."

"Okay but what's his name?"

Dementia slowly gripped the old man. There was no one on the video call. It was just him and his phone's front camera.

CHAPTER FORTY-NINE

THE ARGUMENT

A fierce dispute was taking place in the court of logicians and prophets of love. The logicians were busily scrutinizing true love with their critical eyes. The prophets, on the other hand, took a more holistic approach, arguing that love transcends analysis and cannot be put under the knife.

"True love is mystical, divine, subjective, and most importantly unconditional."

The logicians were petrified as they lacked a cogent rebuttal to the idea of love's unconditionality.

"What if the only condition for unconditional love was to have no conditions at all?"

The room fell silent. The weight of this argument tumbled the hearts and minds. Everyone was deafeningly quiet.

CHAPTER FIFTY

The Realization

Detective Robin Goodfellow, facing a macabre, grotesque crime scene, plagued by bewilderment and confusion. He swallowed his anxiety pills, seeking solace. Delving deeper into the web of clues, he discovered the lifeless body devoid of struggle. His gaze fell upon the victim's hand, clutching a small box full of anxiety pills but poisoned. He sarcastically laughed at the naivety of the killer. A startling, chilling realization washed over Robin when he met the corpse's eyes. It was his own reflection staring back at him. He had unwittingly become both detective and victim in this sinister game.

www.ingramcontent.com/pod-product-compliance
Lightning Source LLC
LaVergne TN
LVHW041100150826
845673LV00007B/1856

* 9 7 9 8 8 9 1 3 3 4 9 8 4 *